JOE SEALBY

Crimson Pursuit

Copyright © 2024 by Joe Sealby

All rights reserved. No part of this publication may be reproduced, stored or transmitted in any form or by any means, electronic, mechanical, photocopying, recording, scanning, or otherwise without written permission from the publisher. It is illegal to copy this book, post it to a website, or distribute it by any other means without permission.

First edition

This book was professionally typeset on Reedsy.
Find out more at reedsy.com

Contents

1	The Crimson Lotus	1
2	Kenji	16
3	Infiltration	34
4	A New Lead	48
5	The Interrogation Gambit	62
6	A Tightening Vice	76
7	Closing In	86
8	Rei Akira	96
9	A Vengeful Vow	112

1

The Crimson Lotus

The sharp crack of gunfire echoed through the street. People screamed and scattered in all directions, the previously bustling sidewalk turning into a chaotic scramble. The operative's instincts kicked in, his hand immediately moving to his holstered pistol. His eyes darted towards the source of the commotion — a man in a dark trench coat was sprinting away, clutching a briefcase, with two armed pursuers hot on his heels.

The agent's earpiece crackled to life. "Target identified," his handler's voice came through. "That briefcase contains critical intel on the Crimson Lotus syndicate. Do not let it escape."

Adrenaline surged through him as he bolted after the fleeing man, weaving through the panicked crowd. The man glanced back, his eyes widening as he the operative gaining on him. Desperate, he shoved pedestrians aside, causing further pandemonium.

The chase led them through narrow alleys and across busy intersections, the neon lights flashing in a blur. The agent's heart pounded, but his mind remained focused. This was his chance to get closer to the Crimson Lotus, and he couldn't afford to let it slip away.

As they rounded a corner, the man in the trench coat stumbled, dropping the briefcase. The agent seized the opportunity, diving forward and snatching the case just as the pursuers caught up. A fierce firefight erupted, bullets ricocheting off the walls. The agent took cover behind a parked car, returning fire with precise shots.

The pursuers were skilled, but this agent's training gave him the edge. One by one, they fell, leaving him standing alone amid the carnage. He quickly checked the briefcase, confirming it held the intel he needed.

With the immediate threat neutralized, the man melted back into the crowd, the briefcase securely in hand. His mission had just become more urgent—and infinitely more dangerous. The Crimson Lotus would stop at nothing to retrieve what he now possessed.

The man's mind raced as he considered his next move. He needed to get this briefcase to a secure location and analyze its contents. He stashed it behind a bin - how secure- and marked the location on his device. This could be the break Interpol needed to finally bring down the elusive syndicate.

As he disappeared into the night, he knew the stakes had never been higher. The hunt for the Crimson Lotus had taken a decisive turn, and there was no turning back now.

The pulsing neon signs cast a kaleidoscope of colors across the rain-slicked streets of Tokyo, reflecting off the dark puddles that dotted the pavement. Despite the late hour, the city hummed with an electric energy that never seemed to sleep.

Cars streamed endlessly down the main arteries, their headlights cutting through the humid night air like knives. Pedestrians jostled down the sidewalks in a hurried shuffle, most with their faces buried in their phone screens, oblivious to the dazzling lights and towering skyscrapers around them. Billboards as large as city blocks flashed rapid-fire advertisements for the latest tech gadgets, J-pop sensations, and lurid energy drinks promising to keep the city's hard-working salarymen powering through their punishing corporate hours.

Weaving through this bright, chaotic landscape was a continuous river of humanity — businessmen rushing home from their offices, packs of rowdy tourists gawking at the brilliant scenery, and solitary homeless men hauling their worldly possessions in battered shopping carts. But amid this dense crowd moved another type entirely, one that went largely unnoticed in the late-night blur of activity.

In a narrow alley between two towering skyscrapers, a solitary figure in a crisp black suit moved furtively, keeping to the shadows cast by the harsh neon glow. His face was obscured by the low pull of his cap, but his eyes scanned the area with a focused intensity, missing no detail of the surroundings. Reaching into his jacket pocket, he pulled out a small device that projected a holographic display only he could see.

The device showed a detailed map of the district, highlighting his location with a pulsing red dot. Several other dots flickered nearby — surveillance nodes he had carefully planted in key locations over the past few weeks. Tapping one of the dots brought up a real-time video feed showing an underground parking garage swarming with burly men in expensive black suits, their wrists adorned with glittering gold watches that cost more than the average Japanese citizen's annual salary.

He zoomed in closer, his eyes narrowing at the sight of sleek, glittering luxury vehicles lining the garage — Bentley, Rolls

Royce, Maserati, and other super-luxury marques. Cars owned only by the ultra-wealthy elite...and the ultra-criminal. This was the place.

The Black Pearl Casino.

Slipping the holographic projector back into his pocket, the man checked the sleek black pistol holstered at his side before ducking out of the alley. He merged seamlessly into the flow of pedestrian traffic, just another anonymous face in the late-night Tokyo crowd.

But despite his carefully unassuming appearance, this man was no ordinary citizen out for a stroll. His name was Hiroshi Tanaka, and he was one of Interpol's most accomplished and elite deep undercover operatives.

From a young age, Hiroshi Tanaka exhibited a decisive intellect and physical prowess that marked him for recruitment into Interpol's elite training program. Even among that rarefied group of candidates, he excelled at marksmanship, mixed martial arts, deductive reasoning, and high-risk extractions under the most extreme forms of duress. But most importantly, Hiroshi possessed an implacable moral resolve that could never be bent or broken, no matter how dicey or dangerous the operation became.

By his late twenties, Hiroshi had already undertaken dozens of high-stakes undercover assignments infiltrating major criminal enterprises all across the Asia-Pacific region. He had penetrated the Yakuza's notoriously insular money laundering rings in Osaka, disrupted Iranian nuclear arms trafficking operations in the hostile borders of Pyongyang, and taken down a nefarious Manila-based drug cartel that brutally tortured informants and enemies alike in gruesome ways.

Each mission saw Hiroshi slipping into deep cover and gradually insinuating himself into the innermost circles of these illicit organizations. Through an unshakable combination of nerves of pure-tempered steel, preternatural abilities at subterfuge and deception, and absolute mastery of combat skills, he had proven time and again his unparalleled talents at infiltration.

Hiroshi's daring methods and unbroken track record of success infiltrating criminal enterprises had built him an elite reputation within Interpol's hallowed ranks. But it had also exacted a price - that of being forced to shed any semblance of normal life and human connections. Any friends, family members, or loved ones were kept at arm's length from his clandestine existence, never privy to the perilous work that consumed him. Apart from his handler back at headquarters, he trusted no one, ever vigilant that betrayal could come from anywhere at any time.

Not that he would accept it any other way. The harsh, solitary vagabond existence was a sacrifice Hiroshi willingly embraced, sworn to rid the world of those who operated without conscience or compassion. Through his years in the field, he had seen firsthand the monstrous depths of depravity people could descend to in pursuit of profit and power. Each horrid sight he witnessed birthed an unquenchable, raging thirst for justice that burned within him like an inferno.

Which was what brought him to Tokyo tonight, stalking the shadows of the nocturnal megalopolis in pursuit of the criminal cabal called the Crimson Lotus. In the prior weeks, he had gradually infiltrated their far-reaching operations, meticulously tracking the syndicate's incredibly diverse range of illicit revenue streams - money laundering, human trafficking, weapons smuggling, and more. All trails, intelligence reports, and financial data pointed to the Black Pearl casino as a central hub where the Crimson Lotus conducted their activities serving Tokyo's wealthiest criminal elite.

Hiroshi knew that if he played his cards right at the Black Pearl's baccarat tables and VIP lounge spaces, perhaps he could catch a glimpse of the syndicate's famously reclusive leadership ranks. Just a single misstep from one of their operatives, one whisper of information inadvertently revealed, and he could potentially start pulling at the first threads that would unravel the entire deadly web of the Crimson Lotus...straight to its insidious heart.

Intelligence gathered by Interpol and law enforcement agencies across the Pacific Rim painted an increasingly chilling portrait of the Crimson Lotus syndicate - a sprawling, multi-national criminal empire engaged in a bewilderingly expansive array of illicit enterprises.

At its core was an elite cadre of highly-trained operatives who executed everything from weapons trafficking to human smuggling with ruthless, military-like precision. But this was just the outer layer of the syndicate's activities. As analysts continued monitoring the Crimson Lotus, they uncovered evidence of its involvement in billion-dollar money laundering schemes, sophisticated cybercrime and digital fraud on a massive scale, and even corporate extortion and industrial espionage against legitimate multinational corporations.

What made the Crimson Lotus particularly formidable was its embrace of cutting-edge tactics and technologies to obfuscate its sprawling illicit operations. Unlike the vain, ostentatious displays of the old-school Yakuza who relied on showy violence and garish territorialism, the Crimson Lotus maintained an unwavering low profile and discipline. Its members diligently covered their tracks behind the banality of legitimate business fronts, obscuring their criminal enterprise through an intricate, constantly shifting web of dummy corporations and shell companies spanning multiple international jurisdictions.

The operatives themselves didn't advertise their activities with the usual criminal gaudy trappings - no flashy suits, garish body art, or ostentatious jewelry. Instead, they blended seamlessly into the civilian population, disguising their true identities behind the facades of ordinary careers and lives - businessmen, civil servants, technicians. Only by removing this impenetrable veil of banality could law enforcement even begin to disrupt their covert operations.

The technological tools employed by the Crimson Lotus to aid in its obfuscation efforts were just as cutting-edge and insidious - encrypted communication networks, blockchain-powered payment gateways laundering money through anonymous cryptocurrencies, and even highly-guarded schematics for 3D-printed weapons and firearms that could circumvent authorities.

The sophistication of the Crimson Lotus' tactics and tools rivaled that of a multinational corporation...or even a nation-state's intelligence agency. Toppling such a formidable foe would require superior resources, manpower, and strategy.

That was why dozens of Interpol's most elite agents and analysts from across the globe had been handpicked to lead the operation to dismantle the Crimson Lotus syndicate, an effort code-named "Crimson Typhoon." It amounted to the largest coordinated offensive against transnational organized crime in the agency's history, with tactical teams deployed covertly into every country and region where the syndicate was known to operate.

Hiroshi Tanaka was at the tip of that spear in Tokyo, tasked with the critically important mission of locating the Crimson Lotus' reclusive and mysterious leader - the woman known only as "Rei Akira." All evidence suggested this brilliant criminal mastermind made her clandestine headquarters somewhere in Japan's capital, carefully insulated within the uppermost ranks of the syndicate's hierarchy.

If Hiroshi could get close enough to identify Rei Akira and her inner circle, it could provide the clue that allowed Interpol to finally unravel the entire deadly web...

By all accounts from intelligence gathered, Rei Akira was a meticulous strategist and cunning tactician who outmaneuvered her adversaries with almost preternatural ease. She deployed the Crimson Lotus syndicate's vast resources - financial, technological, human - with the cold, calculated precision of a grandmaster strategizing every move on a chessboard decades in advance. No matter how solid the operational plan against her organization, Rei always seemed three moves ahead, her latest gambit already anticipated and countered.

What's more, she inspired an almost fanatical devotion among her subordinates in the Crimson Lotus, the kind of zealotry only exhibited by members of pseudo-religious cults or terrorist sleeper cells. Those arrested during raids on the syndicate's safe houses, fronts, and facilities followed a strict ethos of silence and secrecy. They would endure torture and even carry out grisly ritual suicides rather than divulge any information about their enigmatic leader's identity or whereabouts.

It was this meticulously cultivated shroud of mystery surrounding herself that formed one of Rei Akira's greatest advantages. By remaining a faceless, unknowable specter, she rendered herself virtually un-trackable and unpredictable - an ominous presence that terrified her adversaries precisely because so little could be known about her motivations or next move. Each new intelligence brief only deepened the sense that the Crimson Lotus syndicate was akin to a mythological hydra. Lop off one head and two more would grow in its place under Rei's direction, more fortified and sophisticated than before.

The few concrete details about Rei Akira gleaned from interrogation reports and electronic surveillance painted a chilling portrait of a criminal strategist operating on a broader, more ambitious scale than anything previously encountered in the underworld. Unlike the Yakuza bosses of old drawn to petty conflicts over territory and street rackets, Rei harbored grander, more intricate designs. Her overarching vision was to build the Crimson Lotus into a globally integrated financial empire capable of executing any illicit operation from the shadows while staying virtually untraceable to authorities.

To this end, the syndicate's activities under her leadership spanned the entire spectrum of transnational organized crime - weapons trafficking, human smuggling, narcotics production and distribution, illegal cybercrime and financial fraud, corporate extortion, and industrial espionage. Each lucrative revenue stream flowed through a series of sophisticated money laundering operations that filtered the proceeds through a labyrinthine web of legitimate business fronts and shell companies spanning multiple international jurisdictions.

What's more, Rei recognized the need to fully integrate cutting-edge technology and modern white-collar subterfuge into the Crimson Lotus' DNA, further separating her vision from more conventional criminal organizations.

Compounding the threat Rei Akira posed were the indications from intelligence reports that she obsessed over the arcane Japanese myth of the "Crimson Lotus" - an elixir of immortality so powerful, it could only be cultivated by bathing the roots of the sacred lotus plant in the blood of a thousand virtuous souls. While it remained unknown whether Rei truly put credence in this gruesome legend or merely adopted its baroque imagery and mystical symbolism, it was undeniable she had woven the "Crimson Lotus" ethos into a near-religion of sorts among her syndicate operatives.

Members incorporated deep crimson lotus insignias and stylized floral patterns into everything from their encrypted communications and corporate branding to their elaborate body art tattoos. This cultic reverence for their leader's grand "Crimson Lotus" manifesto was most evident during raids when captured operatives recited arcane mantras about metaphysical ascension and murderous "rebirth" before attempting ritual suicides if cornered.

Such all-consuming, quasi-mystical fanaticism woven into the Crimson Lotus' cultural fabric hinted at Rei Akira's powers of meticulous psychological indoctrination over her subordinates...as well as her potential for widespread psychopathic delusion. This was not a mere criminal enterprise seeking profit and power, Interpol analysts warned. Rei Akira's ambitions seemed to be spiraling into the realms of messianic villainy, marked by a grandiose determination to destabilize the established global order itself through escalating acts of orchestrated chaos, violence, and depravity.

This was why bringing Rei Akira's reign to an end took precedence over all other operations for Interpol across the Pacific Rim. The growing dossier on the Crimson Lotus syndicate's expansive reach, technological sophistication, and apparent apocalyptic ambitions under its mastermind leader sent shockwaves through international law enforcement circles. This triggered the launch of the multi-national "Crimson Typhoon" mission.

Only by identifying and severing the syndicate's leadership could its countless deadly tentacles be prevented from further tightening their stranglehold around the globe.

Despite weeks of patient undercover work infiltrating the high-stakes baccarat tables and VIP lounge at Tokyo's Black Pearl casino, Hiroshi Tanaka had yet to make any tangible breakthrough regarding the upper ranks of the Crimson Lotus syndicate. The underground gambling den served as one of the major money laundering fronts for the criminal organization's activities in Japan's capital region. But the identity of Rei Akira and her top lieutenants remained frustratingly obscure, carefully insulated behind the Black Pearl's layers of secrecy and security.

Night after night, Hiroshi played the role of the wealthy but careless Japanese businessman "Akira Mori" to the hilt, his undercover persona now fully accepted into the Black Pearl's inner circle of high-rolling degenerates. Slamming back overpriced whiskeys and chain-smoking pungent Cohiba cigars, he engaged in drunken banter about imaginary business deals and marital woes as he lost and won huge sums at the baccarat tables. All the while, he surreptitiously studied the behaviors and patterns of the other patrons looking for any deviations that could indicate ties to the Crimson Lotus leadership.

The Black Pearl itself played into the delirious fantasies and excess of Tokyo's ultra-wealthy criminal elite. Hidden beneath a nondescript 1980s office building in the heart of Shinjuku's notorious Kabukicho red light district, the subterranean casino was accessed via a discreet entrance staffed by stone-faced Japanese men in tailored Nomura suits acting as security. After passing scrutiny at the entrance, a private elevator coded with daily-changing digital keys whisked patrons down several floors to the main gaming hall of the Black Pearl casino.

Within, the Black Pearl spared no expense in catering to the hedonistic whims of its elite criminal clientele. Burnished cherry wood panels covered the walls, offset by plush burgundy carpeting and low-smoldering lantern lights that cast an air of mystery and exclusivity. The sultry, smoky scent of premium cigars and perfume wafted through the air, mingling with the constant clacking of chips, whirring of slot machines, and occasional raucous cheers from the heated baccarat tables.

Impeccably dressed kimono-clad hostesses slinked between the gaming areas, refilling drinks and providing discreet "personal entertainment" to any high roller willing to slip them a wad of yen notes. A separate secluded lounge area featured deep leather couches, an open bar staffed by kimono hostesses, and a dimly lit alcove where younger female escorts catered to more lascivious appetites.

By all outward appearances, the Black Pearl was simply Tokyo's most exclusive den of debauchery - a lavish, decadent playground where the ultra-wealthy criminal class could indulge in their ogni vice away from prying eyes and scrutiny. But Hiroshi knew better than to be fooled by such superficial veneers. Beneath this facade of bravado and indulgence slithered the viper of the Crimson Lotus syndicate.

He started picking up on the coded phrases and subtle hints after just a couple of weeks of ingratiating himself into the

Black Pearl's social scene at the baccarat tables. The hushed asides and furtive glances whenever someone new arrived in the private gaming rooms. The scrutiny the casino's staff gave to all patrons, keenly judging their legitimacy and wealth. But most telling were the figures who moved like wraiths between the back hallways and secluded chambers, their motions guarded and demeanor far more sober and serious than the inebriated revelry surrounding them.

At first, Hiroshi merely cataloged these movements and encounters, making detailed notes while surreptitiously recording video and audio through micro-cameras and bugs he had carefully planted throughout the Black Pearl's main areas. But then he started overhearing snippets of conversation and coded phrases that piqued his interest:

"The clients are coming in from Kita tonight..."

"Did you hear about the new shipment arriving at the docks from Shenzhen?"

"Lady Azalea should be very pleased with the merchandise we acquired..."

Cryptic phrases laced into casual conversations between carefree patrons that could mean anything in isolation. But for Hiroshi's trained ear, each seemed to hint at something much bigger related to the Crimson Lotus syndicate's far-reaching smuggling operations based on context and intelligence reports.

Each time he overheard such whispers, Hiroshi made sure to slip away under the pretense of "business meetings", leaving the Black Pearl temporarily to consult securely with his Interpol handlers. Meticulously analyzing the data feeds from his surveillance devices cross-referenced against the latest coded intelligence briefings, the layers of the Crimson Lotus' operations slowly began taking shape.

The "clients arriving from Kita" likely referred to a high-level delegation of syndicate members coming in from the organization's stronghold up north along the borders of Akita Prefecture. "Shipments arriving from Shenzhen" almost assuredly meant illicit goods being trafficked into the Port of Tokyo from China - likely narcotics, weapons, or even human cargo knowing the syndicate's breadth of activities.

But the recurring reference to this enigmatic "Lady Azalea" was particularly intriguing. Hiroshi and his team went back through all communication intercepts and surveillance logs, searching for any other potential hits on this heretofore unknown codename. What they uncovered formed a tantalizing trail of breadcrumbs suggesting this "Lady Azalea" could potentially be a vector to the leadership epicenter of the Crimson Lotus itself.

The first clue was financial - records of large transactions funneled through a series of shell companies and offshore accounts all linked to a holdings firm called "Jade Lotus Investments" based in Singapore. Further digging into this company's listed corporate officers revealed it was merely an obfuscating legal entity formed to obscure the true ownership and beneficiaries behind it.

However, one of the authorized signatories for Jade Lotus Investments was listed as using the codename "Dame Azalea" in encrypted communications with other suspected Crimson Lotus operations and fronts across Southeast Asia, particularly in the major illicit trafficking hubs of Kuala Lumpur and Penang. This "Dame Azalea" appeared to occupy a high-ranking role, overseeing many of the syndicate's smuggling routes across the South China Sea and into Japan.

Next were the scattered intelligence reports gathered from

interrogations of captured Crimson Lotus operatives and communication intercepts. Multiple sources referred to a particularly ruthless female operative code-named "Lady Azalea" who carried out enforcement and coordination roles for the syndicate across the Pacific Rim. Her movements and activities were tracked along routes commonly used to smuggle contraband between Southeast Asia, Taiwan, South Korea, and ultimately into Japan for distribution.

While never directly implicated in the intelligence reports, the pieces suggested this "Lady Azalea" potentially occupied a high-ranking position in the Crimson Lotus' leadership hierarchy based out of Tokyo. If Hiroshi could somehow make contact or locate her, it could provide an entry vector straight into the heart of Rei Akira's deadly inner circle.

Of course, discovering the identity of "Lady Azalea" and her role within the Crimson Lotus hierarchy would be no easy feat, Hiroshi knew. The upper ranks of the syndicate were insulated through multiple layers of disciplined secrecy, enforced by a ruthlessly clear code: any breach of operational security would be dealt with through brutal termination.

As he continued mingling in the Black Pearl's inner circle of high-stakes gamblers and dissolute criminals, Hiroshi kept his senses on high alert for even the slightest hints or clues that could start unraveling the mystery surrounding "Lady Azalea." A single misstep, a solitary revelation, and he could finally begin pulling at the threads that composed the tightly woven fabric concealing Rei Akira and her illusive inner sanctum.

2

Kenji

Hiroshi Tanaka scanned the dimly lit casino floor, his eyes narrowing as they adjusted to the hazy clouds of smoke drifting through the air. The Black Pearl lived up to its underworld reputation - a den of iniquity catering to Tokyo's criminal elite. He smoothed the lapels of his tailored suit, adopting the casual confidence of someone who belonged among these vipers.

His gaze settled on a corner table, partially obscured in shadows. A lone figure sat hunched over a laptop, fingers flying across the keyboard. Hiroshi sidled up to the table, appraising the hacker's hooded face briefly illuminated by the glow of the screen.

"Kenji, I presume?" Hiroshi said in a low tone.

The hacker started, his shoulders tensing before he caught sight of Hiroshi. A lopsided grin crept across his lips.

"Fancy meeting one of Tokyo's top operatives in a den like this," Kenji said, leaning back in his chair. "To what do I owe the honor?"

Hiroshi slid into the vacant chair opposite Kenji, keeping his voice pitched low to avoid eavesdroppers.

"I'm tracking chatter about a new player muscling into Tokyo's underworld - the Crimson Lotus crew. I need a hacker, someone to dig up intel where I can't."

Kenji's gaze sharpened with interest as he processed the request. "The Crimson Lotus, eh? Yeah, I've heard whispers. Big-time arms dealers, if the rumors are true. U thought they were still a blip outside Tokyo, but it seems they're growing quicker than expected."

He scrutinized Hiroshi for a moment, giving a subtle nod. "All right, you've piqued my interest. Truthfully, my current employers have been...let's just say unethical even by my standards. I'm game to lend my services, for a price."

Hiroshi allowed himself a thin smile, extending his hand to cement their agreement. Kenji met his grip, his calloused palm betraying his life's work behind a keyboard.

"Let's make it worth your while then. I need all the intel you can dig up - identities, locations, operations. Anything that can unravel their whole syndicate."

Kenji bobbed his head in assent, already sliding his laptop closer with an eagerness that bordered on obsession. His fingers blurred over the keys, screens rapidly flickering with lines of code.

"You've come to the right guy. I'll crack any firewall, and lay bare all their dirty secrets. Just say the word if you need anything specific."

With Kenji beginning his digital reconnaissance, Hiroshi's senses prickled as he turned his attention back to the casino floor. Scanning the crowd, his instincts warned of threats potentially lurking among the well-dressed patrons. He needed to project an air of nonchalance to avoid drawing unwanted attention.

"Let's grab a drink while you work," Hiroshi murmured to Kenji. "We'll make a nice inconspicuous pair of high-rollers."

Kenji snorted, not looking up from his rapidly scrolling screens. "You've got money to burn on overpriced watered-down drinks?"

"My employer's dime," Hiroshi said with a tight smile.

Leaving Kenji to his rapidly evolving cyber-trail, Hiroshi waved over one of the casino's roving waitresses. "Two old Tokyu malt whiskies, neat," Hiroshi ordered in a low voice.

The waitress flashed a smile that didn't reach her eyes. As she sashayed through the crowd to fetch their drinks, Hiroshi leaned closer to Kenji.

"I want you watching for any signs we've been made. Shuffle our secure channels in case we need to cut comms and run."

Kenji's focused expression flickered as he processed the request. He must have realized the dangerous reality of who they were pursuing.

"You think Crimson Lotus has eyes in this pit of snakes?"

Hiroshi gave a grim nod. "I'd bet my life on it. That's why we need to lay low and gather what intel we can before they–"

His words caught in his throat as a familiar face emerged from one of the private lounges adjacent to the main floor. Even across the densely packed casino, there was no mistaking her raven hair and the predatory way she surveyed her surroundings, as if daring any soul to cross her path.

"That's her," Hiroshi hissed under his breath. "Rei Akira herself – the head of the Crimson Lotus."

In an instant, Kenji abandoned his laptop, lips pressing into a taut line as his gaze tracked the infamous crime boss. Rei Akira dominated the room through sheer force of presence, her hourglass figure hugged by a shimmering crimson gown.

She moved through the casino's energetic pulse with cold disregard, trailed by an entourage of burly bodyguards sized like heavyweights.

Hiroshi felt his pulse spike as one of Rei's serpentine eyes seemed to find him despite the crowd. Her full lips curled with derision as if sniffing out his deception like a wolf.

Then, their brief locked stare was shattered by the waitress returning with their drinks. Hiroshi fumbled for his wallet, eyes cutting back to where Rei had been standing only to find she had vanished as inscrutable as a ghost.

"We need to move," he said in a low, tense voice, shoving a wad of bills into the waitress's hand. "Now."

Kenji was already closing his laptop and surging to his feet with a nod of grim understanding. As they hastily retreated, Hiroshi's jaw set grimly, knowing their chase after the Crimson Lotus had potentially turned into a life-or-death hunt.

Rei Akira's blood burned as she watched the two strangers beating a hasty retreat from her casino den. Though she prided herself on an aloof, unshakable demeanor, something about the man in the tailored suit had struck her like a current of electricity. Those eyes... There was a keenness, an intensity simmering behind them that set her instincts on edge.

Who was this interloper to her Black Pearl palace of sin? More importantly, what did he want with the Crimson Lotus?

Rei was no fool - she had forged an empire from the ashes through sheer grit, cunning, and a killer instinct that never slept. Anyone sniffing around her operations was a threat to be extinguished with extreme prejudice. She tracked the two men with a raptor's focus as they hurried out into the neon-drenched Tokyo night.

"Ren," she said in a low, silken voice that nonetheless cut through the casino's noise.

One of her hulking bodyguards seemed to materialize from the shadows at her elbow. "Yes, Akira?"

Rei's gaze remained locked on the rapidly vanishing figures. "Put a tracker on them. I want to know every breath they take, every insect they disturb in this city."

The bodyguard gave a deferential bow, a bark of acknowledgment muffled in the din. As he moved to mobilize the operation, a beautiful woman in a formfitting black dress seemed to condense from the shadows beside Rei. Her makeup was stylishly severe, framing dark, knowing eyes that glittered like polished obsidian.

"Trouble in paradise already?" The woman's voice was a practiced purr, hinting at untold secrets.

Rei allowed herself a faint smile, sipping from a glass of deep crimson wine. This was her protege, her latest recruit from the disbanded remnants of the Yakuza clan. For now, she would play the role of enigmatic mentor.

"Snakes often slither into the garden, Emi," she mused. "We simply trim them back before they can spread their venom."

The protege arched one delicately manicured eyebrow at the veiled response. Already, Rei could see the younger woman's keen intelligence dissecting her words, analyzing every inflection and micro-expression like an artist studying a masterwork's brushstrokes.

Good. Cultivating such insight would serve her well in time.

"And if they slither in from an unexpected corner?" Emi pressed. "What then?"

Rei's smile turned predatory, sanguine lips pulling back to reveal a glimpse of gleaming fangs.

KENJI

"Then we shed a little blood to ensure our blossoms yield only the most perfect crimson lotus."

As Emi absorbed the dark metaphor, Rei's eyes traced an unhurried path back toward the entrance where the two men had fled. A muscle ticked in her jawline, the only hint of percolating menace behind her impassive mask.

Let them try to scurry from her sight. She possessed resources that could track a shadow through the labyrinth heart of Tokyo itself. No, the interlopers hadn't escaped her grasp - not by a long stretch. They had merely wriggled onto her hook, where she could savor reeling them in at her leisure.

Rei allowed herself a predatory smile as the first ember of her grand machinations sparked to life. If these two foolish little mice insisted on scurrying into her lair, so be it.

Her Crimson Lotus's roots would soon strangle this city's underbelly in a blinding crimson embrace. And then, with Tokyo bent to her dominance, the entire world would shudder as she unfurled her petals to drink in the sun.

After all, every lotus grew from blood-soaked depths. Hers would be no exception.

Hiroshi's breath came in ragged gasps as he and Kenji hurtled down the neon-drenched streets of Tokyo's entertainment district. His pulse thundered in his ears, adrenaline spiking as shadows seemed to lurk in every alley and doorway they passed.

"Did we lose them?" Kenji wheezed, throwing a furtive glance over his shoulder.

Hiroshi shook his head grimly. "Not a chance. Rei Akira doesn't let her prey slip away that easily."

His eyes raked their surroundings, searching for any signs of pursuit amidst the crowds spilling from hostess clubs and karaoke bars. At first glance, it was just the normal nocturnal chaos of pleasure-seekers and drunken salarymen looking to blow off steam. But Hiroshi's instincts warned of the deadlier predators potentially circling, just waiting to move in for the kill.

"This way," he muttered, grabbing Kenji's arm and pulling him down a narrow side street.

They plunged into the shadowy backstreets, the cacophony of Tokyo's main drags fading to a dull throb. A few stray souls huddled in doorways nursing bottles in crumpled brown bags, but otherwise the passages were deserted at this late hour. Hiroshi's steps slowed, senses straining for any sound out of the ordinary.

Kenji opened his mouth, perhaps to ask what their next move should be, but Hiroshi held up a hand to silence him. Narrowing his eyes, he detected a flicker of movement ahead - the barest distortion of shadows detaching from a recess in the brickwork. With a sinking sensation, he realized they had been herded right where their hunters wanted them.

Without a word, Hiroshi shoved Kenji into a narrow alcove, using his own body to shield the hacker just as a hail of bullets shredded the night air. Concrete exploded in a shower of shrapnel inches from Hiroshi's face as he tucked into cover, teeth gritted against the ringing in his ears.

Two black-suited figures stalked from the shadows ahead with military precision, semi-automatic rifles leveled and sweeping in search of their targets. Hiroshi recognized the attackers' distinctive shark-like masks - henchwomen in Rei Akira's elite Crimson Guard.

"Now would be a great time for some of those skills you were bragging about, Kenji," Hiroshi growled over the deafening gunfire.

To the hacker's credit, Kenji took several calming breaths and reached into his jacket to extract a streamlined metallic cylinder. With a subtle hand motion, he unsheathed a telescoping antenna and twisted a dial on the side that cast an infrared beam into the darkness ahead.

The attack drones - virtually invisible in the night - became searing afterimages of heat signatures converging on their position.

"Ever the masters of subtlety," Kenji muttered under his breath, rapidly keying commands into the cylinder's illuminated control panel.

A metallic whine shrilled through the air as the drones' propulsion systems seized, plummeting them to the pavement in a clatter of carbon fiber and servo drives. The Crimson Guards halted their barrage in momentary confusion at the sudden equipment failure. It was all the opening Hiroshi needed. With a primal shout, he erupted from cover, body carving through the air as he closed the distance in a blur. He struck the first assailant dead center with a vicious sidekick, the impact slamming her into the opposite wall with bone-shattering force. Already twisting on the balls of his feet, he seized the rifle from the second attacker, wrenching it away even as she squeezed the trigger reflexively. The hail of bullets screamed a lethal spiral up into the night sky.

The henchwoman gasped in shock at her weapon being ripped away so easily. That lapse in composure cost her dearly as Hiroshi unleashed a devastating flurry of strikes - fist snapping her head back, knee crashing into her ribs, foot sweep whipping her legs out from under her. She toppled in a boneless heap, mask cracked and already drifting toward unconsciousness.

Silence descended over the alley once more as the echoes of combat faded. Hiroshi straightened, gaze sweeping for any further threats. Behind him, Kenji emerged from the cover with a low whistle of impressed awe.

"You, uh, don't mess around much, do you?" The hacker eyed the fallen henchwomen strewn like broken dolls.

Hiroshi tossed aside the rifle, already searching the defeated foes for any clues. "Don't mistake me for some reckless punk brawler off the street," he muttered. "Rei Akira's people are killers, and she'll send more until she gets what she wants."

His fingers closed around a metallic shard from an earpiece discarded amid the wreckage. Tracing its sleek contours, he detected a blinking LED indicator no bigger than a pinprick. Hurling it away in disgust, the tiny tracker smashed against the alley wall into useless shrapnel.

"Only a matter of time before more of those disposable killers track us down," he said grimly, turning his gaze toward the distant glow of Tokyo's skyline. "Now you see why we can't stop - not until we cut off the Crimson Lotus's corrupted head."

Kenji swallowed hard, nodding with a new sense of resolution. He tapped commands into his cybersecurity cylinder, scanning the airwaves for any further traces of their location being compromised.

"Whatever these Crimson freaks have planned, we have to shut it down. Fast." He fell into step behind Hiroshi as the operative set off once more into the labyrinthine maze of Tokyo's backstreets and alleys.

Despite successfully evading their initial pursuers, Hiroshi felt the night's darkness pressing in all around them. They were little more than rats scurrying through Rei Akira's domain now. Judging by the ferocity of her opening salvo, the snake would not rest until she had located her trespassers and devoured them whole.

The predawn streets of Tokyo had fully surrendered to the shroud of night. Under the veil of darkness, the city's pulsing neon arteries turned into a disorienting labyrinth of shadows and secrets.

Perfect camouflage for those who lurked in its underworld underbelly.

Hiroshi stayed in a perpetual coiled crouch as he and Kenji pressed deeper into the tangled maze of alleys and side streets. Every footfall was measured, each sweep of his gaze searching for potential threats - a flicker of movement, a glint of metal, even the barest hint of a shadow out of place. After the brutal ambush from Rei Akira's elite Crimson Guards, he knew it was only a matter of time before she sent further forces in pursuit.

"How are we looking?" he muttered under his breath.

Kenji's face was bathed in the sickly glow of his cybersecurity device as he monitored the airwaves. "Quiet for the moment," the hacker murmured back. "But your snake lady isn't one to give up easily by the looks of it."

A wry smile turned the corner of Hiroshi's lips at the moniker, though the expression never touched his eyes. "No rest for the vicious, as they say..."

He gestured for Kenji to follow as they turned another corner, pressed flat against the brickwork. They moved with the silence of shades, attempting to melt seamlessly into the night itself even as it deepened toward true midnight blackness. All the while the sense of being watched grew more oppressive, like a noose tightening around their necks.

Then the hairs prickled on the nape of Hiroshi's neck - that undeniable sixth sense screaming an imminent attack. He didn't even have to bark a warning as twin pinpricks of crimson light blazed from the shadows ahead, tracing toward them with soulless mechanical precision.

"Laser sights!" he snarled, hurling himself forward and seizing Kenji by the collar.

The alley around them erupted with the demonic chatter of assault rifle fire spraying concrete in every direction. Instinct alone allowed Hiroshi to fling Kenji and himself out of the line of fire a split second before the bullets found their mark. They tumbled hard against the fractured pavement, Kenji letting out a pained grunt as the wind was driven from his lungs.

For Hiroshi's part, his focus locked onto the silhouettes of three more Crimson Guards swinging into view, their shark-like masks gleaming like chromium fangs in the night. One pinned Hiroshi with a sustained burst aimed straight for his exposed skull, the other two fanning out to flank them in a crossfire of sizzling lead.

With no other recourse, Hiroshi snapped his armored forearm into position to deflect the barrage just long enough to pinpoint the source of the laser sights. Following them back, he glimpsed a sniper team perched atop a dilapidated warehouse roof in the distance - their beacons were what had marked Hiroshi and Kenji for execution.

Allowing himself a grim smile, Hiroshi seized hold of the pistol from the small of his back and unleashed a punishing salvo of shots back up towards the rooftop. The snipers scattered in a panic, ruby focus beams fragmenting into frenzied spirals as they scrambled for cover.

It was a momentary distraction...but a moment was all Hiroshi required.

Tucking into a vicious shoulder roll, he surged towards the lead Crimson Guard with lethal speed, unleashing a brutal barrage before her rifle could swivel to track him. A whiplash kick sparked from Hiroshi's heel to slam her weapon aside with a bone-jarring impact. She howled in pain as the merciless assault hammered home - strikes slamming into her throat, ribs, kidneys, and groin. Pressure points blossomed in savage sequence until the resilient henchwoman finally crumpled in a heap, choking on her blood and defeat.

   There was no time to linger on the victory, as Hiroshi spun to confront the final two assailants rushing to flank them. Moving with the fluid grace of a salaryman dodging through a packed commuter train, he weaved through their roaring gunfire like an eel. Getting inside the arc of their attack, he kicked one rifle into the air on its upward recoil, sending it spiraling into the shadows. With the other he simply seized the barrel with his bare hand, searing agony lancing up his arm as the superheated metal seared his flesh.

   But Hiroshi had been forced to endure far worse torments - such trivial pains were merely gateways to unleash the ferocious berserker lurking within. With a savage snarl, he wrenched the gun free and cracked it across the attacker's skull in a blinding arc. The Guard went down in a boneless sprawl with a choked gurgle.

   As the last standing enemy faltered at the abrupt shift in momentum, Hiroshi had already closed the gap with frightening intensity. The Shark Mask's frantic attempts to fend off his blurred flurry of strikes were pitiful at best. A kick sparked ribs like dry timber beneath the Guard's body armor. A hammer fist snapped her head to the side, spraying bloody spittle to hiss across the scorched pavement. And finally, a brutal knee to the abdomen folded her body in half, collapsing in a heap just like her compatriots.

It was over in the space of mere breaths - the battle won with ruthless, surgical violence. A sepulchral hush draped over the alley once more as Hiroshi straightened, breathing hard yet controlled, the stance still coiled to strike. His obsidian gaze swept the area one final time before allowing himself a nod of satisfaction.

Only then did he turn to where Kenji remained huddled against the wall, staring with a mixture of awe and sheer terror. The hacker seemed to recoil even further when their eyes met as if facing down the merciless specter of death himself.

Hiroshi held his gaze for a lingering moment, forcing himself to soften the intensity of his feral demeanor. In a low voice, he spoke the first words to pierce the haunted stillness.

"Are you unhurt?"

After an uncertain pause, Kenji managed a mute nod. Relief seemed to seep back into his tensed muscles as he rose on trembling legs and made his way toward Hiroshi with exaggerated care.

"They... They are out for blood." The hacker's voice was faint, senses no doubt assaulted by the intimacy of a life-or-death battle paid in bone and viscera.

"Now you see why stopping the Crimson Lotus is job one," Hiroshi spoke calmly, impassive mask descending once more. "Rei Akira will not stop sending her rabid attack dogs, not until she has torn both of us limb from limb."

Kenji followed the sweep of Hiroshi's gaze across the motionless Crimson Guards strewn around them. The shock and horror appeared to fade from the hacker's eyes, replaced by a grim understanding of the stakes they faced.

"Then we'd better make sure that hellion burns before she can unleash any more of those demons on us."

Hiroshi allowed a thin smile to ghost across his lips. The chase had only just begun... but at last, he had lit a fire to purge the darkness in this young hacker's heart.

Soon, Rei Akira and her entire empire would face a reckoning blazing hotter than the bowels of Dante's Inferno itself.

Hiroshi kept one eye trained on the maze of backstreets while the other scrutinized Kenji furiously working his hand-held cybersecurity device. The hacker's brow was furrowed in intense concentration as lines of code flickered across the screen, occasionally punctuated by a muttered curse.

"Well?" Hiroshi's gravelly tone betrayed barely-leashed impatience. "Were you able to lock onto Rei Akira's signal before we had to ditch the tracker?"

Kenji shot him a sidelong glance, clearly ruffled by the operative's abrupt manner even after the life-or-death battle they'd just endured. To be fair, the hacker's hands still trembled slightly from the trauma.

"Give me a second, will you? I'm doing my best, but that woman's got safeguards and encryptions layered like crazy"

Hiroshi opened his mouth to retort but quickly snapped it shut again. As much as every instinct burned to strike back while the element of surprise remained, antagonizing his only tech support would be a foolish strategy. They were both invested in this now, like it or not.

He settled for giving a terse nod and resuming his patrol of their temporary haven - a long-abandoned machine shop tucked into one of Tokyo's countless hidden alcoves. Thick steel shutters shielded the entrance, for now offering sanctuary from

Rei's relentless trackers while they regrouped.

Minutes ticked by in tense silence, the only sounds to be heard were Kenji's muted muttering and the occasional rattle of debris being shifted under Hiroshi's watchful footsteps. The operative circled the perimeter again and again, keen eyes sweeping for any hint of a breach while the rest of his senses remained on high alert.

Finally, Kenji broke the silence with a grunt of triumph. "Gotcha, you serpent..."

He looked up to find Hiroshi immediately at his side, expression carved from unforgiving granite.

"Talk to me."

Kenji's throat bobbed in a reflexive gulp before he launched into a rapid debrief. "Like I said, that Rei chick doesn't make things easy. She's running a virtual merry-go-round of proxy servers and kill switches to cover her trail."

He paused to wipe a sheen of sweat from his brow, expression pinched with the weight of the challenge he'd been grappling against.

"But she can't hide from me entirely. I managed to piggyback a ricochet trace to isolate her core security node, then de-crypt the location data before she vaporized it all."

A tap of his finger spun a three-dimensional holographic display to hover in midair - a wireframe schematic of Tokyo's industrial waterfront district rendered in eerie blue light. A single pulsing red node indicated the cracked mainframe.

"This is the source," Kenji declared, staring hard at Hiroshi to gauge his reaction. "My best estimate puts Rei's main weapons manufacturing and storage warehouse right... there." He pointed to a warehouse by the port.

The warehouses loomed large in the neon-tinged projection

like ominous leviathans crouched beside the swelling tide of Tokyo bay. Fitting, Hiroshi mused, that her viper's nest would slither below the waves but strike out across the city's jugular shipping channels.

For a long moment, the operative simply studied the hologram grinding through scenarios in his mind's eye. Strategic ingress vectors, anticipated counter-measures, potential hostage situations, deployed assets required... Each element is rapidly calculated and shelved for future consideration.

At last, his volcanic eyes lifted to meet Kenji's gaze. The hacker tensed, poorly masking his discomfort even now at the intensity smoldering in those obsidian depths. The corner of Hiroshi's mouth twitched in a fleeting semblance of a smile.

"Not bad work," he understated in that trademark gravelly rasp. "Looks like we found our new path straight into Rei Akira's heart of darkness..."

Inclining his head in a subtle nod, Hiroshi turned on his heel and strode back towards the shadowed workbenches lining the machine shop. Hanging on pegs were an assortment of well-worn tools and implements - wrenches, clamps, even an ancient chain hoist that had seen better decades. But Hiroshi's focus locked onto a battered steel locker standing against the back wall.

Without a preamble, he planted a vicious kick into the abused door, metal groaning in protest. Again his boot crashed home, hinges finally shrieking as the locker toppled backwards in a plume of dust to reveal its contents...

An armory's worth of lethal munitions and high-tech gear.

Swiftly yet methodically, Hiroshi began breaking seals and checking systems, shoulders rolling in anticipation. Nearby, Kenji hovered in a mixture of awe and trepidation at this latest glimpse of the resources being brought to bear.

"You, uh, didn't mention your backers being that well-equipped..." he hedged carefully.

Hiroshi barely registered his words, deftly checking a matte-black pistol's sight and swapping in a fresh magazine. He finally deigned a cursory glance over one shoulder.

"We go in with everything we can muster. Anything else is suicide."

He could sense Kenji struggling to reconcile the gravity of the battle lines now being drawn. No more thrilling underworld chase, no more dodging gangster pawns. They were about to strike at the very heart of an arms-dealing empire, at a woman who had already proven herself utterly without mercy.

Lives would be lost. Blood would soak the ground. Such was the price of heroics in this depraved world. But actions like these, on nights like this, were the only path to pave over such ugliness in the first place.

At last, Hiroshi stood fully upright, his armaments checked and tactical gear donned with practiced confidence. He turned at last to fully face the wary hacker.

"You've stuck by me this far, Kenji. Part of me respects your courage in that much... But I won't underestimate you by sugar-coating what's to come."

He held the other man's gaze in silence, letting the weight of reality settle in.

"There will be killing. Ruthless killing, by my hand if need be. If this mission means slaughtering Rei Akra's entire criminal empire down to the last thug, then so be it."

Hiroshi's voice carried no inflection - neither relish nor hesitation. He spoke with the same matter-of-fact tone as remarking on the weather. Whether Kenji had the stomach for it or not, this was simply the burden they shouldered.

To Kenji's credit, he managed to meet Hiroshi's foreboding stare without flinching. His jaw worked as if tasting something bitter, then seemed to find his resolve.

"You got it, man," he said, squaring his shoulders. "Just tell me where to aim my magic fingers next, and I'll burn this whole Crimson shtick to the ground if I have to."

A grim smile tugged at Hiroshi's lips as he jerked his chin in a brusque nod. It was as much approval as the hacker could likely expect from such a stoic, hardened killer.

They gathered their arsenal in silence, mentally steeling themselves for the onslaught to come. Kenji would lay the digital trail ablaze in a hurricane of cyber wildfire, disorienting and disrupting Rei Akira's operations from every encrypted corner. And Hiroshi, would plunge into the incandescent inferno itself, weapon in hand to cut out the Crimson Lotus's beating black heart once and for all.

3

Infiltration

The pre-dawn stillness hung heavy over the warehouse district, the cavernous spaces between rusted hulks of metal looming in the shadows. An eerie quiet blanketed the deserted loading docks and vacant lots strewn with debris - the silence before a gathering storm.

Hiroshi moved through the desolate landscape like a wraith, his footfalls making no sound on the cracked asphalt. The dark lenses of his tactical goggles scanned unceasingly, flicking through thermal optics and motion tracking as he advanced deeper into the waterfront sector Kenji had pinpointed. According to the hacker's trace, this decaying industrial zone by the docks served as one of Rei Akira's major weapons storage and distribution hubs for fueling the Crimson Lotus syndicate's arsenals.

A harsh whisper crackled in Hiroshi's earpiece, Kenji's coded voice cutting through the tense silence.

"I've got full access to the port's security grid now. Looks like Warehouse 17B should be our target - major heat bloom and a surveillance blackout over that sector."

INFILTRATION

Hiroshi allowed himself a grim smile as his enhanced vision locked onto the structure in question through the shimmering haze of heat distortion. The steel hangar-like structure sat alone in a desolate clearing littered with rusted shipping containers and skeletal crane arms reaching toward the night sky. Not surprising Rei's soldiers would centralize operations in such an isolated pocket away from prying eyes and security sweeps.

"Any signs of our friendly welcoming committee?" he murmured back.

A few seconds passed before Kenji's reply came. "Negative. At least on the exterior. But you can bet the snake definitely has this place locked down tight from within."

Hiroshi grunted an affirmative, having expected as much. His gaze turned skyward, scrutinizing the lattice work of crane arms and corroded pipes crisscrossing above along the roof of the warehouse. An infiltration option was taking shape, providing a stealthy vector past the first layers of external defenses.

"Keep those eyes peeled for any surprises while I work my way inside," he ordered Kenji in a low voice. "Time to see what deadly toys our viper has stashed away in this den of hers."

Moving with the patiently coiled intensity of a panther stalking prey, Hiroshi picked his way through the ruins of the derelict port toward a gnarled fire escape clinging like a rusted ribbon to the side of the warehouse. Below, the vast structure loomed dark and silent. But Hiroshi's combat-attenuated senses warned of the potential for any number of sinister surprises lying in ambush beyond those unseeing walls.

He began his ascent with slow, methodical care, boots finding purchase on each buckled landing with a natural climber's grace. Within thirty seconds, he was scaling the final perilous spans toward the jagged precipice of the warehouse roof. Below, the corroded metal skeleton of a burnt-out crane provided the only audible chorus, its relic pieces groaning in the faint downdraft swirling off the bay.

Reaching the rusty lip of an access hatch, Hiroshi paused to run one last thermal sweep. There - the unmistakable mercury bloom of multiple warm bodies milling in the subterranean chambers below. So the proverbial snakes did lurk within their nest, just as expected.

With a subtle tap of his mic, he brought Kenji back online in a hushed murmur. "I'm set up topside with eyes on target. You're clear to initiate support overwatch whenever you're ready."

A beat of silence passed before the reply crackled back. "Roger that. I'll start squirming my way into their systems on your mark." Hiroshi could practically taste the grim eagerness behind the hacker's voice, like a sprinter awaiting the starter's pistol. For all his self-professed social awkwardness, Kenji seemed to relish the role of remotely disemboweling Rei's operations from within.

Hiroshi felt his own pulse spike in anticipation as he crouched over the roof hatch, senses pitched toward any hint of detection. This was it - the tipping point when all preparation gave way to action, no matter how dire the circumstances ahead. He drew a final, steadying breath, ensuring that every reflex and combat discipline was honed to absolute perfection. Then, with a subtle click of his jaw, he spoke the single code word that would unleash their assault:

"Scorched Earth."

In that instant, Hiroshi's world erupted in a kaleidoscopic maelstrom of light and sound. An electronic shockwave of force seemed to roll across the warehouse grounds as Kenji initiated his cybernetic onslaught. Security systems began wailing and industrial lighting banks flickered in seizure-inducing strobes.

Through the chaos, Hiroshi maintained lazer-focused discipline, slamming his hand onto the roof hatch release while the other snatched his suppressed sidearm from its holster. As the hatch shrilled in protest, he dropped into a crouch with the ease of an oil-slicked piston, weapon raised to acquire targets through the haze of sparking electronics below.

Three silhouetted figured immediately burst into view from the smoke and haze, shouting in alarm and leveling their own weapons towards the breach. Hiroshi didn't give them time to react further, his own fire already thundering with mechanical precision. Crimson mists bloomed in sync with each muted report as his accelerated rounds found their marks with cold accuracy. The first hostile spun backwards with a gruesome exit wound, the second knocked spinning from the force of impact trauma. The third managed a single wild burst before Hiroshi's next double-tap caught him square between the eyes, abruptly silencing his final gasped cry.

In the span of mere heartbeats, three more of Rei Akira's pawns lay unmoving amidst scattered brass casings.

Maintaining his coiled firing crouch, Hiroshi took a single second to assess the new landscape through his thermal optics - a charnel house of cooling bodies untidily strewn about a dimly lit central staging area. Row after row of wooden pallets, munitions crates, and shipping containers surrounded the open space, forming a lethal maze in every direction as far as his visor could see.

Shouting echoed from deeper within the shadows, along with the pounding of running footsteps and slamming of chains as Rei's forces were no doubt mobilizing to reinforce the breached outer chamber. Hiroshi knew he had a brief window to seize an advantageous foothold before the inevitable counterattack.

In a rapid series of hand signals coded into Kenji's cyber uplink, he pinged their coordinated assault plan: provide suppressing fire across the room to allow him to secure a hardened fallback position. Without waiting for an acknowledgment, Hiroshi rolled into motion, sidearm barking toward deeper shadows even as ricochets sparked around him.

Hunkering behind a fortified crate, he maintained a withering field of fire as weapon discharges erupted from multiple converging angles through the haze. To their credit, the Crimson Lotus soldiers reacted with coordination, immediately saturating the area with overwhelming volleys from multiple firing positions spread throughout the warehouse.

With his off hand, Hiroshi was already keying his cybernetic grenades, altering their compositions for maximum lethality. Hurling the first two spheres into the densest killzone vectors, they erupted in blinding magnesium flashes and concussive sonic booms that momentarily shocked and disoriented the hostiles in those sectors.

Immediately, he followed up by tossing an armor-piercing explosive charge into a chokepoint to allow Kenji's entry. When it detonated in a catastrophic roar of overpressure and structural debris, it ripped open a stretch of caved-in ground that even the battle-hardened Lotus troops would balk at trying to mount an assault through.

Sure enough, in that temporary lull before the next surge of violence, Hiroshi caught sight of Kenji scrambling through the ragged breach firing rapid bursts from an automatic shotgun, its integrated 40mm grenade launcher raining down suppressing salvos of buckshot and smoke canisters. They regrouped behind a stout cement pillar supporting the warehouse's skeletal framework, backs pressed against the solid surface while pouring counter-fire in all directions.

"Welcome to the party," Hiroshi growled to the hacker, lip twisting in a mordant grin. "I was starting to think punctuality wasn't your strong suit."

Kenji's face was sheened in sweat and eyes were wild behind his goggles, but he offered a breathless chuckle in return.

As if to accentuate his nonchalance, an armor-piercing round cratered off the pillar inches from his head, showering them both with pulverized concrete shrapnel. Kenji let out an undignified yelp, hunkering tighter.

"So...any big ideas for getting us out of this slice of hell, samurai?" he yelled hoarsely over the screaming cacophony of gunfire reverberating through the chamber.

Hiroshi maintained his steely calm, thumbing a fresh magazine into his sidearm and chambering a round with a well-practiced twitch of his wrist.

"First we deal with this little resistance faction. Then we take the fight straight to their master before she slithers off into whatever hole she's dug..."

Another piercing round sheared clean through the pillar, this one missing Hiroshi's skull by mere centimeters. His teeth glinted in a savage grin, the thrill of violence singing through his nerves and heightening his predatory senses.

"Just the way I like it - good and bloody."

The staccato thunder of gunfire echoed through the cavernous warehouse, round after round crunching into the fortified pillar shielding Hiroshi and Kenji. Splinters of concrete shrapnel slashed at their faces as they hunkered behind the rapidly deteriorating cover.

"I hope you've got another trick up your sleeve!" Kenji shouted over the deafening barrage, desperately punching commands into his combat rig's tactical systems. "Because these psychos really don't want us crashing their weapons party!"

Hiroshi allowed himself a feral grin at the hacker's understatement. From the moment they'd breached the warehouse's outer security cordon, the Crimson Lotus soldiers had waged a relentless counterattack, hammering their position with overwhelming firepower. At least a dozen of Rei Akira's red-armored elite occupied hardened firing positions throughout the facility, steadily constricting a lethal killzone around the two infiltrators.

"Just keep those firewalls solidified," Hiroshi growled back, thumbing a fresh magazine into his weapon with cold precision. "I'll make us an exit..."

Not waiting for a response, he burst from cover in a spinning helix, sidearm thundering repeated bursts toward the heaviest concentrations of hostiles arrayed against their position. Immediately, Kenji unleashed a torrent of suppressing fire from his automated assault shotgun and grenade launcher, sheets of shredded steel and high-explosive shrapnel saturating the battlespace.

The maelstrom of violence allowed Hiroshi to rapidly acquire footholds, using towering stacks of crates, heavy cargo pallets, and fortified alcoves as a deadly assault lattice. He was a spectre of smoke and death itself, phasing in and out of scant cover with lethal precision while scything down any Crimson Lotus fighter reckless enough to be caught in his killing fields. Rifle bursts sparked against a crate on his left only to be answered by a hammering fusillade that stitched the shooter's combat armor with fist-sized exit wounds. A grenade detonation bloomed on his right, demolishing an elevated sniper's nest in a thunderclap of fire and shrapnel.

Every piece of ground painfully ceded by Hiroshi's overwhelming onslaught merely fueled his lust for greater violence, propelling him deeper and deeper into the heart of the warehouse. He moved with an almost preternatural sixth sense, every combat discipline and martial talent honed to their sharpest razors as he cut a wide swath through Rei Akira's defenses. This was his element, his blood singing with the hot metal chorus of war towards its crescendo.

By the time Hiroshi finally slammed his back against a munitions cache near the central logistics area, ten more of the red-armored Crimson Lotus soldiers lay strewn in cooling pools of viscera throughout the cavernous space. His pistol's barrel smoked faintly in the hazy air, the stench of burnt cordite and ruptured flesh thick as a miasma.

A moment later, Kenji skidded into position beside him, green tech-ribbons still flickering across his visor as he fed constant updates into their tactical network. His shoulders heaved with deep, gulping breaths and Hiroshi could make out the faint tremble in the hacker's limbs - the aftershocks of his first soul-searing baptism of blood and fire.

"Animal...you're an animal out there, you know that?" Kenji's words emerged strained, features still sheened in sweat behind his goggles.

Hiroshi cracked a grim smile at the assessment, slapping a fresh magazine home and racking the slide of his weapon. Above them, the vaulted ceiling arched towards a spiderweb of suspended cargo and loading ramps where the last of the Crimson Lotus holdouts continued to concentrate their defenses.

"Only one way to deal with animals…" he murmured. "And that's to put them down."

Drawing a calming breath, he made a series of rapid-fire hand gestures toward Kenji, conveying the next stage of their assault plan. The hacker's eyes narrowed at first in incomprehension before widening as he processed the audacity of the maneuver. With a short nod of grim determination, he mirrored the signal to confirm and readied his systems.

Moving in perfect synchronicity despite the cacophony raging around them, the two combatants burst from their hasty cover in perpendicular vectors, every motion precisely coordinated and overlapping. Kenji immediately saturated the remaining firing zones with a blanketing salvo of anti-personnel shredders, tracers crisscrossing in angry crimson streaks toward any heat signatures registering as hostiles. At the same time, his free hand seamlessly fed micro-commands to his cybernetic rig, rapidly reprogramming sections of the warehouse's suspended gantries to start shifting erratically on their servos.

The sudden chaos caused the Crimson Lotus gunners to waver as their carefully prepared firing lines splintered in confusion. That split-second lapse was all Hiroshi needed to capitalize on the havoc, his own line of advance taking him straight up a steep stairwell to the elevated loading platform using the lurching cargo machinery as intermittent mobile cover.

At the apex of the ramps, a squad of Crimson Guards waited with rifles trained, unleashing disciplined lances of fire toward Hiroshi's ascent. But the operative never broke stride, body twisting in a sinuous spiral to evade the stream of tracer paths burning toward him. In one motion, he launched himself into a furious midair somersault, legs crunching against the helmet of the lead shooter to catapult him up and over onto the platform.

Hiroshi hit the ground in a crouch, sidearm already blazing with measured two-round bursts that dropped two more hostiles before they could break from their stunned stupor. The rest finally reacted, pivoting to acquire their target, but Hiroshi became an unstoppable red blur of destruction - shattering knees, fracturing arms, crushing larynxes with each precisely measured strike, all the while continuing to weaponize lethal forward momentum.

In the span of fifteen heartbeats, what had been an organized firebase of elite Crimson Lotus commandos lay in a broken, smoldering ruin at Hiroshi's feet. He straightened, shoulders rolling like a panther shaking off the blood and chaos of the hunt.

In the sudden stillness below, Kenji emerged from his fortified position advancing into the logistics staging area. His armored boots crunched and on the ground from the wake of Hiroshi's onslaught.

"Just a few more warm bodies for the pyre," the hacker called out with a hint of morbid relish. He gestured with his rifle toward one of the loading bays, where the reinforced cargo door had been blown open from the inside.

Seconds later, a lithe, swaying strut sauntered into view beneath the paltry lighting, shapely hips and toned limbs accentuated beneath the skintight body glove of faintly glimmering armor. As the figure stepped fully into the open, Hiroshi narrowed his eyes at the mocking expression and ruby-tinged lips that greeted them.

"Well, well..." the woman's voice fairly dripped with arrogant condescension. A lock of fiery azure hair spilled over one eye, the other coldly taking their measure. "Rei did tell me to prepare for some...vermin infesting our operations."

She regarded Kenji with a sneer before fixing her imperious gaze upon Hiroshi above. A heartbeat of tension passed between them, sizing one another up - two alpha predators aiming for dominance.

Only after allowing her smirk to linger on the precipice of outright provocation did the woman finally speak again, each word drawn out with elaborate precision.

"My name is Emi... And I'm afraid our little engagement has only just begun."

The haughty figure continued strolling forward with a predatory sway of her hips, each footfall slow and measured as if savoring their first fateful encounter. Behind her, two more crimson-armored Crimson Lotus troopers emerged with weapons leveled, forming an arrogant escort.

"You've caused quite the impressive massacre down here," Emi sing in a voice laced with dark amusement. She deliberately trailed one fingertip along the shredded obliteration surrounding them as if inspecting a masterwork canvas.

Up above on the loading platform, Hiroshi felt his muscles subtly tense in anticipation of further violence to come. There was an unnerving edge to this woman, a sense of coiled menace simmering behind that mocking facade. His instincts warned of her being something more than simply another Crimson Lotus thug, regardless of her bravado.

"I'd ask if you were enjoying your welcome party," the woman continued languidly. "But I rather suspect you're the type who prefers to let your actions speak louder than words."

Hiroshi allowed the insult to roll off him, stance remaining coiled and uncompromising. Below, Kenji shifted his weight, the hacker clearly rattled by their seeming disadvantage with the two crimson-clad soldiers forming a crossfire angle against them.

But then a familiar sardonic grin stretched across Hiroshi's lips, catching Emi's eye. She arched one slender eyebrow inquisitively at the operative's amusement.

"My actions thus far have really just been the opening salvo," Hiroshi called back down, his deep gravelly voice reverberating through the warehouse. "But please, by all means...feel free to continue providing even more targets to riddle with a few thousand more holes."

Emi's ensuing laughter pealed out like a wicked bell, clear and scornful. "Oh I like the bravado! Although we'll see if your bite can truly back up such brash words, little man."

With a subtle flick of her wrist, the two red-armored troopers began tracking their weapons toward Hiroshi's elevated firing position. But before they could even settle into proper stances, a cyclone of whirling steel fury erupted amid them in a shrill whine of servos and renting metal.

One of the suspended loading gantries - its guidance system still reprogrammed from Kenji's earlier hack - erupted into a spastic seizure of thrashing robotic limbs and whipping cables. The nearest Crimson Lotus trooper didn't even have time to register surprise before being smashed aside, his rib cage compacting with a wet crunch. His partner reflexively spun to engage the violent machine threat, only to be entangled in a coil of hydraulic cabling that lacerated his jugular in a thick spurting arc.

The mechanical maelstrom lasted mere seconds before subsiding just as abruptly, leaving scatterings of mangled wreckage surrounding Emi's lone silhouette. She regarded the corpses at her feet with an expression of stoic dispassion for several taut seconds.

"Well..." she purred at last, once more facing Hiroshi. "It seems your little friend has a few neat parlor tricks after all."

Before Hiroshi could respond, she preemptively held up one hand in a placating gesture, shaking her head in gentle admonishment.

"But I'm afraid our audiences must be cut short for now. Rei will be most displeased if I don't tend to her needs before our other guests arrive later this evening."

Despite the playful, almost seductive tones, there was something vaguely ominous about her reference to these "guests." Hiroshi's grip tightened fractionally on his pistol, but he forced himself to remain impassive, sensing an opportunity taking shape.

"By all means then, don't let us keep you," he called back in an arid deadpan. "I'm sure we can find some way to...occupy ourselves until you're done playing dress-up with your friends."

Emi's laughter rang out through the warehouse again, this time carrying an edge of genuine mirth. She angled her head to one side, eyeing Hiroshi with an approving allure.

"My, my...such flirtations from a man who was just drowning this room in oceans of blood." She clicked her tongue in mock-reproach. "Almost makes a girl forget which of us is supposed to be the villain."

With a final, dismissive sweep of her eyes over Kenji's position below, Emi spun on one heel and began retreating back toward the loading bay entrance. Each sashay of her hips seemed to carry a palpable dare. But Hiroshi held his fire, waiting until the sultry vixen's silhouette finally vanished once more into the shadows.

The moment Emi disappeared, Kenji blew out an explosive sigh of relief below. "What the hell was that all about?" he muttered in a strangled tone, still reeling from their surreal encounter.

Hiroshi kept his eyes trained on the empty doorway, senses tuned for any hint of treachery yet to come. When several beats of silence ticked by undisturbed, he finally allowed himself to relax a fraction.

"That…" he murmured down to Kenji, "would be our opening to finally get a peek behind Rei Akira's crimson curtain."

Slinging his pistol, Hiroshi began meticulously making his way back down the precarious walkways and stairwells littered with debris. As he reached the main level, Kenji hurried to join him, his optics scanning the operative for further explanation.

Hiroshi regarded the hacker for a moment before speaking, voice lowered in grim contemplation.

"There's more going on here in this pit of snakes than just weapons manufacturing and trafficking. Rei's whole organization seems to be building toward something… bigger. Something more nefarious on a scale we've not even grasped until now."

His fist clenched, fresh determination etching across the granite planes of his features.

"And that female viper Emi seems to be our potential Gordian knot for unraveling the whole twisted mess. Find out who she is, what her connections to the Crimson Lotus's larger operations are, and we may just have a way to get inside Rei Akira's sanctum and cut off this entire viper den's head once and for all."

4

A New Lead

The echoes of gunfire and Emi's taunting laughter still rang in Hiroshi's ears as he and Kenji surveyed the devastation surrounding them. Corpses of Crimson Lotus soldiers lay twisted and broken amid the shredded wreckage of loading equipment, a brutal monument to the violence they'd unleashed.

"You really think that arrogant snake-hipped viper is our ticket into Rei's inner sanctum?" Kenji murmured, gingerly prodding one of the dismembered crimson-armored bodies with the toe of his boot. "She seemed awfully confident. Dangerous."

Hiroshi frowned, jaw clenching as he considered the hacker's words. There was no denying the unnerving power and poise that had radiated from Emi's every movement. The way she'd mocked them amidst the slaughter, utterly undisturbed by the carnage...it spoke of something more than mere bravado.

"Overconfidence often breeds arrogance," he replied after a moment. "And arrogance leads to flaws that can be exploited. We'll start digging into who - or what - Emi really is and what her role is within the Crimson Lotus hierarchy."

His obsidian eyes bored into Kenji's with an intensity that burned hotter than any furnace. "Because you're right - she's our most direct channel to Rei Akira right now. And I have a feeling if we can unravel the secrets surrounding her, we'll expose the heart of this entire poisonous operation."

Kenji seemed to shrink slightly beneath that scorching emerald stare before giving a resolute nod. "You're the boss on this insane thrill ride," he muttered, already feeding commands into his tech rig to initiate protocols. "If that Red girl back there is our best shot at the end boss, then let's see what nasty Easter eggs are hiding in her code."

Leaving the hacker to his virtual machinations, Hiroshi began methodically searching the perimeter for any additional clues or intelligence that may have been overlooked in the heat of battle. His combat scanner panned over every scrap of debris, every potential data-point analyzed and catalogued for later analysis by Kenji's systems.

After several minutes of meticulous examination, Hiroshi paused beside a burned section of wall pocked by bullet impacts. There, tucked behind a half-collapsed stack of pallets, lay the shattered remains of a red-trimmed combat helmet bearing three jagged claw-mark insignias along its breached faceplate. The coloring and insignia immediately registered as belonging to a Crimson Lotus elite shock trooper.

Bending down to scoop up the damaged helmet, Hiroshi felt its heft and studied the catastrophic breaching pattern along the reinforced cranial armor. Even at a cursory glance, it was evident the damage had been caused by a concentrated barrage of incredibly accelerated projectiles - likely from an armor-piercing ballistic weapon.

Kenji glanced up at the operative's scrutiny of the helmet,

brows furrowed. "Find something useful?"

"Not sure yet," Hiroshi admitted, continuing to turn the fractured crimson headgear over in his grip. "But the localized damage patterns don't match anything we deployed." He indicated the intricate web of micro-punctures scoring the interior cranium plate. "This was done by a rapid-fire high-velocity weapon far exceeding even military-grade small arms. Something with incredible force projected over an extremely confined muzzle arc."

Realization dawned across Kenji's features as he ran an analytical scan of the cranial trauma. "You're saying it was caused by some sort of organic railgun system?" His lips twisted in a grimace.

Hiroshi's expression remained impassive, but he gave a curt nod of affirmation. "That's my theory at least. A biological railgun-type ability like that is on a whole other level of power. A level of power which would fit right in with the upgraded elite trooper class we faced today."

Letting the shredded helmet drop back to the debris-littered floor, Hiroshi straightened and began pacing in contemplation. "If Emi has tactical assets with that level of organic ballistic augmentation at her disposal, it could explain her utter disregard for niceties after our initial clash." His eyes narrowed to emerald slits as the implications congealed.

"She knew she was holding something back - some ace still up her sleeve that we have yet to glimpse. Which begs the question..." he trailed off, staring pointedly at the hacker, "why not finish us both off right then and there if her forces were so superior?"

Kenji opened his mouth to retort - then promptly shut it, head tilting as he mulled over the operative's words. After a few moments of contemplation, he gave a helpless shrug. "Because like you said - arrogance, right? Why waste the big guns on a couple of insignificant bug splats like us if she can just punt us aside for later?"

"Or..." Hiroshi pressed, his tone becoming grim with certainty. "There's something bigger going on here that even Emi and her elite shocktroops are just one small part of. Something being orchestrated by Rei and her upper echelons at a scale we still can't fathom..."

A heavy silence hung between the two men as they considered the terrifying implications of that scenario. Images flashed through Hiroshi's mind, fragments of intelligence gathered over years of counter-operations against the Crimson Lotus: whispers of world-shaking plans set into motion by Rei Akira, sightings of strange black technology at their converted sites, even rumors of biomechanical experiments and augmentation programs conducted on human test subjects.

Every time the shadows had seemed on the verge of coalescing into something tangible, the conspiracies had slithered back into the murkiest depths before the truth could ever be exposed. But now, it felt as though they were finally standing on the event horizon of something far more catastrophic than a mere crime syndicate's weapons operation.

Squaring his jaw, Hiroshi turned his inflexible stare back toward Kenji. "We're going to find out what game is really being run here. Take that helmet back to your sanctum and have every bioscan analysis you can drum up run on it. I want to know exactly what manner of monstrosities we're dealing with in Rei's new elite hierarchy."

The hacker reacted instantly to the no-nonsense orders in the operative's tone, scooping up the ruined headgear and beginning to rigorously document it for transport. "You got it," he muttered grimly, all traces of his former levity vanished beneath the grim revelations of what they were truly facing. "Time to peek behind the red curtain and see just how deep this bloody abyss goes..."

Hiroshi allowed a mirthless smile to tug at one corner of his mouth as the first steps of their new operation took place. There was something undeniably intoxicating about the thrill of diving headlong into ever-deepening layers of shadow...never knowing when you may have finally plunged too far into the abyss to find your way back to the light.

"Just make sure you have a safety tether rigged this time," he growled softly, more to himself than to Kenji. "Because I have a feeling we're going to need a lifeline back from whatever fresh hellscape we're about to drag into the light..."

Turning on his heel, Hiroshi stalked toward the ruined warehouse's main entrance with a cold sense of determination etching his strides. The hunt was officially on in earnest now, and there would be no quarter given or mercy shown until the prey was finally run into the ground, no matter how deeply its lair may be buried beneath the sins of man's conceits...

Kenji watched Hiroshi's implacable form departing into the shadowed warehouse interior before glancing back down at the shattered crimson helmet cradled in his hands. His fingers traced over the jagged ballistic scars marring its surface, grimacing at the thought of the sheer force required to inflict such catastrophic trauma.

For a moment, a tremor of trepidation caused his grip to falter - the dawning realization that they were now fully ensared in something far bigger and more horrifying than they'd ever imagined. The Crimson Lotus's entire existence seemed to be an intricately woven veil concealing secrets and technologies that shouldn't be possible outside of science fiction.

What new unfathomable horrors might they uncover by peeling back those layers of deception? What fresh terrors had Rei Akira's cabal truly uncaged in their lust for power and domination?

Kenji's eyes slid shut, jaw clenching as he drew a fortifying breath to still the rising doubts - no such trepidations were useless now. They had crossed that bridge the moment they'd set foot inside this warehouse of slaughter and damnation. There could be no turning back, not until the whole vile truth was finally laid bare before the light of justice.

"Hang onto your bucket of nuts and bolts, Red" the hacker murmured, offering one final mocking salute toward the ruined warehouse before turning to follow Hiroshi's path. "Pretty sure the only thing waiting for us at the end of this bloody trail is gonna redefine our definitions of 'madness.'"

Slinging his rifle across his back, Kenji triggered his boot thrusters and arrowed off into the smog-shrouded Tokyo night. His mind was already racing ahead, calculating strategies and contingencies for the maelstrom to come while his tech analysts began meticulously deconstructing their newly acquired crimson trophy.

They had been granted the rarest and most terrifying of glimpses behind the curtain shielding Rei Akira's true maleficent ambitions. And Kenji knew there would be no rest, until that veiled shroud was finally torn away entirely.

No matter how much blood and damnation had to be dragged screaming into the light to make it happen.

Kenji's multiple computer screens flickered with lines of code as his fingers flew across the keyboard. "Got something big," he said tersely, eyes not leaving the displays. "There's an incoming shipment scheduled for tonight at an abandoned dock on the south side."

Hiroshi leaned in closer, trying to make sense of the coded manifests and logistic plans scrolling by. "That's weapon shipment?"

"Has to be." Kenji did a few more commands, and pages of data analyzed the shipment's details. "The quantities and weights match what we'd expect for heavy arms. And get this - I tracked the shipping instructions back to a shell company we know is linked to the Crimson Lotus."

A spark of hope lit in Hiroshi's chest, quickly dampened by hard-bitten caution. "Could be a trap, or just a decoy meant to throw us off Rei's trail."

Kenji shrugged. "Maybe, but it's our first real solid lead in weeks. Way too much effort for a simple decoy." He gestured at the screen. "I mean, look at all the layers of obfuscation and redirection - coded manifests, anonymous front companies, circuitous shipping routes. This has Rei's fingerprints all over it."

Studying the intelligence together, Hiroshi had to agree it looked legitimate. Detailed inventories, shipping container IDs, freight logistics - all linked back to documented Crimson Lotus fronts through the hacker's relentless tracing. Still, his years of field experience prompted extreme caution.

"Okay, we tentatively treat this as an active operation. But we go in quiet and careful as hell. No screw-ups like at the warehouse." The memory of that ambush made his jaw tighten. "We let them make the first move, no shooting unless absolutely necessary."

"You know me." Kenji grinned fiercely. "I'm the reigning

A NEW LEAD

king of quiet and careful."

Hiroshi suppressed an eye-roll at the hacker's overconfidence. That same brash attitude had nearly gotten them both killed last time. But Kenji's cyberwarfare skills were undeniably critical, and they were perilously low on leads to track down Rei Akira.

"The shipment's scheduled to come in around 0200 hours," Kenji said, checking the timeline. "We've got plenty of time to get into overwatch positions and scope it out thoroughly first."

Nodding grimly, Hiroshi felt a surge of anticipation - and no small amount of dread. He had a sinking feeling this operation was going to be a long night. But if this arms shipment really did lead them to the elusive Rei and her high-level lieutenants...

It would all be worth it to bring the Crimson Lotus' criminal empire crashing down in flames.

The pre-dawn hours found Hiroshi and Kenji hunkered in overwatch positions amid the crumbling ruin of Tokyo's south-eastern docks. Rusted cranes stood like watchful giants, while stacks of cargo containers created a neon-lit maze of potential ambush points.

"This is definitely the right zone?" Hiroshi muttered over comms, surveying the seeming emptiness. It all looked deserted, almost too exposed and open for an illicit arms transaction.

"Positive," Kenji's voice crackled in his ear. "Subsection gamma-four, just like my intel said. We're in the right spot, trust me."

Fresh from their warehouse ambush, Hiroshi had hoped to hit a more confined, controllable location this time. Out here in the wide open, any hostile could approach from any angle. He risked exposing himself to get a better view, craning around a cargo container's edge.

The night pressed in, oddly silent except for the occasional cry of seabirds. Then Kenji's voice caught an alert tone. "We've got movement, ten o'clock! Trawler approaching the delta-nine dock."

Snapping his night vision goggles into place, Hiroshi scanned the dark waters until the outline of a rust-pitted fishing boat emerged, cutting through the waves toward a dilapidated dock. As it pulled alongside, over a dozen armed men began swarming topside like ants.

"I count twelve hostiles so far, maybe more below decks," Kenji reported crisply. "Whoever's receiving the shipment must be groundside."

Not the worst odds, Hiroshi calculated grimly, at least if it was just hired muscle rather than Rei's professional killers. But out here, surrounded by open terrain with lines of fire from every direction...any minor edge could turn deadly in an instant.

"Hold for my go signal," he ordered Kenji tersely. "Let them make the first move, then we-"

His words froze as something else appeared in his scope's view, a sleek shape cutting through the waves. Not a rust-bucket trawler, but an unmistakable modern warship bristling with weapon emplacements.

Kenji clearly picked up the sinister new contact at the same moment. "That's no transport ship, that's military-grade offensive...I'm reading peaked energy signatures, EM hardening, classified weapon configs."

A chill gripped Hiroshi's guts. There could be only one explanation. "One of Rei's warships. The Crimson Lotus' best tech and heaviest firepower."

Which also meant the whole operation had been deliberately seeded. That arms shipment was a trap - baited specifically to lure them into this killing field as Rei herself rolled up with overwhelming force.

"You're right," Kenji said, tension clear in his voice. "She knew we were coming all along...played us like a damn fiddle!"

For one frozen heartbeat, cold clarity washed over Hiroshi. Only one possible move remained: take the fight to the enemy hard and fast before they were hopelessly outmatched.

"We're blown," he said flatly. "No more waiting. Hit them with everything you've got before that warship locks us down!"

Without waiting for acknowledgment, he vaulted over his cover in a flat sprint toward the assembled hostiles. His suppressed pistol cracked twice, dropping two bandits with precise blood-blossoms on their foreheads.

On his command, Kenji's cyberdeck unleashed its payload - hurling a trio of micro-drones screaming from their hardcase toward the trawler. Bristling with high-ex munitions, the tiny buzzing hornets streaked through the night to deliver tank-killing fury.

Hiroshi's first two shots were the spark that detonated a conflagration of chaos. Gunfire, screams, the deafening roar of Kenji's drone strikes...and the harsh whine of the Crimson Lotus warship's systems spooling up for attack.

Smoke and flame billowed across the transformed battleground as a firestorm of violence erupted from every angle. The same instincts that had kept Hiroshi alive through a thousand firefights kicked into overdrive as he zigzagged evasively, raking suppressing fire toward every glint of hostile muzzle flash.

Kenji, too, had abandoned any pretense of stealth, his micro-ordnance saturating the area with high-velocity shockwaves as he goaded the enemy warship's tracking systems into a deadly shell game.

In seconds, the abandoned dockyard had transformed into

an inferno of searing battle, steel raining from the skies as the outnumbered agents fought with everything they had to stem the overwhelming Crimson Lotus forces.

Unfortunately for them, Rei Akira was a grandmaster at these sorts of explosive confrontations - and she always played her games for maximal carnage. While her body may have remained offsite, her vicious trap had been sprung with perfect, punishing timing.

As a salvo of warship missiles turned the night into day, Hiroshi and Kenji could only grit their teeth and pray their luck wouldn't run out before they found some way to turn the tide. Because going down in flames wasn't an option - not as long as the Crimson Lotus still cast its poisonous shadow over Tokyo.

Tracer fire criss-crossed the night sky, punctuated by thunderous explosions as the Crimson Lotus warship unleashed its fearsome armaments.

Hiroshi sprinted for what little cover he could find, a burned-out forklift providing paltry protection against the devastating onslaught. "Ideas would be great right about now!" he shouted over the cacophony.

"Working on it!" Kenji's voice crackled through the comms, his micro-drones still swarming evasively to occupy the enemy's targeting systems. "But we're seriously outgunned here. That frigate's no joke!"

No sooner had the words left his mouth than a quartet of missiles detonated nearby, the massive shock wave slamming Hiroshi from his meager cover. He tumbled hard, the wind knocked from his lungs, barely managing to keep hold of his sidearm. Coughing through the smoke and fumes, he forced himself back to his feet, the world spinning.

Only sheer training kept him alert enough to dive aside as another salvo saturated his position with high explosive fury. Chunks of shredded steel shrieked past as he flattened behind a cargo container's shadow.

"Kenji!" No response. Panic spiked as he tried to raise his partner on comms. "Kenji, sound off!"

Static. Then a pained groan echoed from somewhere across the devastated dock. "...here. Ugh, still in one piece I think..."

Relief warred with pragmatism as Hiroshi realized they were cut off from each other amid the firestorm, able to last only minutes more without some kind of miracle. And he was fresh out of those tonight.

Wait...maybe not a miracle, but a gambit just insane enough to work? Squinting up at the warship raining hellfire all around them, he noticed its cannons lowering to reacquire targets. In moments, its full might would simply pound them into red mist.

Except...for one flickering opportunity, if he timed it just right.

"Kenji, new plan!" He switched frequencies urgently. "I need you to launch a level seven virus package at that warship's systems, full system infiltration. But only on my go signal!"

"What?" The hacker sounded as stunned as if Hiroshi had sprouted a second head. "You want me to initiate a cyberattack against one of the Crimson Lotus' most advanced military craft? Are you insane?"

"Probably," Hiroshi admitted with a mirthless chuckle. "But trust me. If we're going down, we may as well make our last stand really count."

A hesitation, then: "You'd better know what you're doing. The package is loading up, ready to deploy on your signal."

Licking his lips, Hiroshi keyed his tactical visor, timing the warship's rotation carefully. Just a few more seconds until its forward cannon barrels swung into blindspot alignment...

"Execute virus upload...NOW!"

As Kenji's cyberstrike lanced out, punching through the frigate's electronic defenses, Hiroshi was already moving. Digging deep into the last reserves of his energy, he sprinted directly at the looming juggernaut, switching his sidearm to fully automatic as its cannon clusters swung blind.

The gambit was insane...and their one thin hope. If Kenji's virus could overwhelm the frigate's systems even momentarily, the narrow window should last just long enough for Hiroshi to capitalise. And if not...

Well, at least they'd depart this world having given Rei's vaunted warship a few new holes to remember them by.

As the deadly cannons swung free, spraying fire blindly into the night around him, Hiroshi leapt onto the railing of a rusted gantry - using it as a launching ramp to project himself straight up onto the frigate's gunmetal flanks. One hand found a precarious grip in the crimped armor as the other emptied what was left of his magazine into the firing slits and seams he could reach.

Unsurprisingly, his pistol did little damage, bullets pinging futilely away. But the desperate stratagem had one other vital effect: confirming his position directly under the main cannon battery's tracking sensors.

"Cover me!" He keyed his mic quickly as the massive gun turrets swiveled back around, their automated targeting software struggling briefly against Kenji's override hack. There was only one chance...

On cue, Kenji's micro-ordnance filled the skies around the warship again, decoying the self-defense cannons into a blistering, sensor-blinding barrage. For an eternal three seconds, the system was blind – and its armored belly was vulnerable.

The ship exploded into an impressive show of light and sound, shrapnel raining into the murky water below.

However, Hiroshi knew full well that this wasn't the end and if they wanted to scorch the Crimson Lotus into the ground, they would need to find Rei.

5

The Interrogation Gambit

The firefight at the docks had been a brutal wake-up call. Hiroshi winced, gingerly touching the bandage wrapped around his ribs as he settled into the saferoom's battered sofa. That ambush could have ended a hell of a lot worse if not for Kenji's cyber-wizardry and his kamikaze gambit. Speaking of Kenji, Hiroshi glanced across the dingy apartment at his partner, the hacker's eyes locked on the flickering screens as his fingers flew across multiple keyboards. "Please don't tell me you're trying to hack a Crimson Lotus warship again. Pretty sure one near-death experience is my quota for the week."

"Relax, I'm not that crazy." Kenji didn't look up from his frantic typing. "Just doing some, y'know, light recon work. Seeing if I can backtrace those ships' deployment data, maybe triangulate Rei's whole hub for this operation."

Hiroshi frowned, leaning forward despite the protesting twinges in his side. "Does something about the weapons shipment intel not sit right with you?"

He could have sworn he detected a slight hesitation before Kenji responded neutrally. "Not really. All the hallmarks were there - the deep obfuscation layers on the logistics, the dummy routing through all those front companies and cutouts, the crazy layering of code and false leads..."

"Exactly," Hiroshi broke in, expression hardening. "So why did the plan feel so sloppy and ill-conceived compared to Rei's usual methods? That whole setup practically screamed 'ambush' from a mile off."

That got Kenji's attention, the hacker slanting him an appraising look across the room. "You think it was a deliberate feint? That she meant for us to sniff out that intel and spring the trap from the start?"

Shrugging gingerly, Hiroshi leaned back with a wince. "I'm not ruling it out. After the way things went sideways at the warehouse too...something about this whole op doesn't add up."

For a long moment, they regarded each other in contemplative silence. Just two shadow agents battered and bruised, well aware they'd nearly danced with the grim reaper once again. All in the line of duty against an enemy who seemed to outmaneuver them at every turn.

"Well," Kenji said finally, turning back to his displays with renewed determination. "Only one way to find out if this was an elaborate gambit or just a stroke of incredibly bad luck." A few more commands flashed up coded data streams and geographic maps. "We dig deeper. Rip away every layer of her deception one by one until we reach the blazing truth at the center."

Hiroshi grunted in agreement, eyeing the hacker's work grimly. At this point, obsessively overanalyzing every angle was about their only recourse. Because if all their efforts to pin Rei Akira were nothing but an intricately woven feint leading them on a merry chase. The criminal queen was toying with them more brazenly than either could have imagined. And for some dark, unseen purpose yet to reveal itself.

The next several days passed in a feverish blur of data mining, gumshoe casework, and dead ends. Behind a rotating array of secured servers and encrypted uplinks, Kenji burrowed ever deeper into the digital layers of obfuscation surrounding Rei Akira's illicit operations. Hiroshi ran the pavement, chasing fragmented paperwork trails and sussing out potential witnesses. Together, they compiled an ever-expanding web of criminal fronts, financial irregularities, and tentative associations branching out from the Crimson Lotus' core leadership. A jigsaw puzzle of Tokyo's dark underbelly…but each promising piece only revealed how many were still maddeningly absent from the bigger picture.

"Just once, it'd be nice if these underworld vultures kept a paper trail that didn't dead-end in scripted accounting errors and bricked cyber-vaults," Kenji growled in frustration, forcibly closing yet another locked-down server farm's access node.

Looking up from the dossier notes he'd been compiling, Hiroshi grunted in weary agreement. "It's almost like Rei has anticipated our every move so far, scrubbing her trail cleaner than a hazmat crew on burnout patrol." Tapping his pen against the pages, he shook his head slowly. "The more angles we run, the more blatant her counter-deceptions become."

"So what, you think she wanted that ambush to happen?" Kenji dragged a hand down his face tiredly. "Sacrificed an entire waterfront op and capital warship just to reinforce her mythic reputation and screw with our heads?"

"You're the expert. But I wouldn't put it past her twisted game at this point." Hiroshi sighed, leaning back to stretch his aching shoulders. "Could be she's scrubbing one set of trails to deliberately gaslight us into chasing decoys while her real plan takes shape behind the curtain."

A heavy silence fell between them, twin warriors battle-weary from pursuing their elusive quarry. The phantom wolf who danced perpetually ahead, laying false trails to lure the hunters ever deeper into her elaborate traps. All pieces on a grand chessboard aimed at some sinister endgame yet to reveal itself.

Watching the frustration of Kenji's expression, Hiroshi felt his own mouth tighten grimly. Because there was another, even darker possibility. One that coiled deep in the pit of his stomach like a viper poised to strike. What if their supposedly solid lead at the docks hadn't been a feint or counter-deception at all? What if Rei had simply surmised their desperation would compel them to blunder into any half-baked clue or ambush she tossed in their path as bait?

It was a galling notion, to be certain. That their years of training and experience could be so effectively neutralized by an adversary playing into their own aggressiveness and resolve to succeed. Just the sort of cruel psychological stratagem Rei Akira would embrace with sadistic zeal to lead them on by their sheer determination until they utterly discarded caution in pursuit of any shadow she trailed before them.

The thought was almost too dire to consider. Because if their relentless hunt was rendering their p predictable, then Hiroshi and Kenji might already be straying from their mission into Rei's insidious checkmate scenario. Her perfectly constructed end game, where the world's elite hunters became the hapless hunted. Just one pawn's stumble from total defeat.

"This is getting us nowhere," Hiroshi growled, surging abruptly to his feet. "We're chasing theories spun from mental vapor trails, not facts."

Kenji looked up, startled by his partner's intensity. "What

do you suggest, then? All our data mining and fieldwork is just running us in circles-"

"Which means we hit the streets again, old-school style." Hiroshi cut him off with a hard look. "Time to press some flesh with the real player elements out there. See if we can rattle the tree hard enough to shake out some genuine leads on what Rei's really been orchestrating."

Grabbing his jacket, Hiroshi checked the grip of his sidearm, tucking it inside his waistband. "Get your go-bag. We're making the rounds tonight - club scenes, back-alley deals, underground hangouts. I don't care if we have to beat down every last yakuza bagman in the city. We're not walking away empty-handed again."

For a long moment, the cyberpunk hacker simply stared at him. Then a slow, predatory smile curved Kenji's mouth as he gave a sharp nod of agreement. "About damn time we stopped chasing shadows and brought the fight directly to their door."

With a few taps of his keyboard, Kenji activated his full suite of combat systems - lethal micro-drones slithering into ready configurations within their armored casings. "Just point me at whoever needs waking up to our respective badassery. I'll make sure they receive the message... loud and clear."

The neon-drenched streets of Tokyo's nightlife district pulsed with energy as Hiroshi and Kenji immersed themselves in the urban underbelly. Glitzy hostess clubs and illegal gambling dens lined the cramped alleyways, their doorways perpetually haunted by roving gangs of Yakuza enforcers and hustlers looking to make a score.

It was the perfect hunting ground to find someone with knowledge of the Crimson Lotus' movements. The hard part would be separating the credible sources from the endless stream of posturing street rats just running their mouths.

"Keep your eyes peeled," Hiroshi muttered, hands jammed in his jacket pockets in a deceptively casual stroll. "We're looking for anyone with heavyweight connects - gang captains, underbosses, illegal guides."

Kenji made a noncommittal grunt, though his eyes never stopped roving, sizing up each cluster of hardened criminals they passed. "Good thing I wore my lightweight body armor then."

Despite the sarcasm, Hiroshi could hear the undercurrent of tension in his partner's tone. For all their years of bleeding-edge hacker experience, Kenji still preferred to tackle obstacles from a remote, cyber-secure remove. Direct confrontation with the Yakuza's street-level food chain definitely wasn't his usual mode of cooperation.

Senses on high alert, Hiroshi scanned the gritty neon-lit alleyways for any potential threats. He'd blended in enough times during past investigations to know that any outward display of anxiety or weakness was an open invitation for violence - the wild dogs could sense fear like a shark scenting blood in the water. Sure enough, the further they delved into the sinister heart of the district's narrow warrens, the more overt the scrutiny became from the loitering patrols. Greasy enforcers sneered out their suspicion, and more than once, groups of leather-jacketed punks made obvious attempts to obstruct their path, shoulders squaring for a challenge. All it would take was one wrong turn or provocative move to erupt into open hostilities.

Ignoring the blatant attempts at intimidation as best he could, Hiroshi kept his eyes roving for any faces that looked promising.

Part of undercover work was having a hunter's instinct for likely allies and assets amid the most unsavory pools of potential victims. There had to be at least a handful of people here with illicit connections deep enough to put them in Rei Akira's orbit.

One particular thoroughfare off the main drag looked ripe as any to start asking questions. Kenji slid a cautious look sideways as a cluster of biker punks huddled outside a decrepit dive bar scowled openly at them. "Uh...you sure you want to risk this particular shark tank? I'm reading major want-to-prove-themselves vibes from over there."

"If they had anything worth boasting about, they wouldn't be squatting in some trough behind a bar, would they?" Hiroshi replied evenly. "C'mon, the kind of real player we're looking for will be-"

"Well now, look at what we have here..."

The mocking drawl rolled from the shadows of the alley mouth as a wiry Japanese man in a cheap burgundy suit slunk into view, half a dozen grinning punks peeling out behind him. Though his finely-coiffed hair and expensive jewelry screamed "big little gangster", there was a canny light glinting in the thug's yellowed eyes.

"Two fresh round eyes come to experience the thrills of the Devil's Elbow," the mobster sneered in English, chortling at some private joke. "Without a local guide, you two're apt to get yourselves all turned around and unintentionally offended."

Hiroshi turned to face him, expression set in neutrally bland lines. "We're not looking for a tame touring experience." His eyes bored into the Yakuza captain with pointed meaning. "Just the most unvarnished and profitable kind."

For a few seconds, there was silence as their gazes locked and the underworld soldier seemed to reassess the situation. When he spoke again, his tone had taken on a slightly more deferential edge. "Profits are a rare commodity around these parts..."

"We're after a rather unique variety," Hiroshi replied meaningfully. "The kind that might just put us in business with the illustrious Crimson Lotus."

The Mafioso's eyes flashed at the name, while his entourage of underlings stirred uncertainly. Taking a half-step forward, he eyed the newcomers up and down with re-calibrated interest.

"Should've recognized the look in your eyes straight-off. You hunt bigger game than the usual gaijin trash sniffing around our district for penny-ante vices and distractions. That is indeed a rare and highly-hazardous commodity you're chasing."

Sliding his hands out of his pockets in a slow, decisive movement, Hiroshi let their steel press through his jacket lining. One wrong move from this vulture would leave them painting the alleyway red.

"Let's just call it our current...occupation. One that could potentially reap dividends to the right kind of facilitator."

A cocky grin curled the gangster's mouth, but his eyes remained calculating. Weighing the potential threat against the possibility of sorely-needed profit, no doubt. These were the kinds of high-stakes gambles that could make or break a minor crook's standing in the larger hierarchy.

"Tell you what, hot-shots..." The kingpin finally purred, rubbing thumb and forefinger together meaningfully. "My boys and I could indeed make certain introductions and arrangements that might be...mutually advantageous. But it'll cost you a lil' up-front incentive to properly grease the wheels."

Any other time, Hiroshi would've scoffed at the naked extortion attempt. But tonight, they needed leverage any way they could get it. Nodding curtly, he pulled out a thick wad of cash, peeling off the top few bills to toss dismissively at the thug's feet. "Half now, the rest on delivery of quality merchandise. Your fee just to get us in the door."

The Yakuza didn't miss a beat, simpering obsequiously as he scooped up the bills. "Such business-minded honor and integrity. You'll find I have great instincts for sniffing out the most rewarding opportunities for those with ambition."

Tucking the cash into his pocket, the gangster spun on one heel with a triumphant smirk. "I'll arrange for transportation to a neutral third-party establishment sometime soon. Have my associates contact you with the when and where..."

As the boss strutted off chortling to himself, tracers of eddying smoke silhouetted his entourage shifting and swarming to follow - a nest of lethal cobras who'd just gotten their first bloody scent. Behind him, Kenji leaned in close, expression grim. "Please tell me you've got a plan here besides courting our own execution? Because I've got a sinking feeling this dirtbag is leading us straight into a Crimson Lotus slaughterhouse..."

Hiroshi's jaw tightened, resolve hardening even as his instincts screamed the same concerns. All he could do was nod as he met Kenji's gaze levelly. "Just make sure to keep your head on a swivel, partner. One way or another, we'll get our hooks into Rei's operation. Even if we have to swim through a viper pit to do it."

Because as the ruthless ambush at the docks had proven, desperation and determination could just as easily transform them from hunters to the hunted in this lethal game of shadows.

The dingy basement room reeked of stale smoke, sweat, and desperation. Hiroshi tried not to pull a face as the thick miasma assaulted his senses, focusing instead on the bruised and battered form of the Yakuza thug bound to the chair before them.

Kenji moved with cold efficiency, slinging another plastic tarp over the floor to catch any spilled fluids or biological detritus. No need to leave unnecessary DNA traces behind. Once he had finished preparing the makeshift interrogation cell, he nodded grimly at Hiroshi.

"Showtime. You want to take lead while I handle the... motivational aspect?"

Hiroshi's mouth tightened ever so slightly. While intellectually he understood the pragmatic need for such extreme tactics, the idea of calculated torture never sat easily. Especially against low-level street muscle who didn't sign up for an anti-crime death sentence.

Still, they were out of options at this point. The greasy mobster had indeed delivered as promised, arranging transport to one of the Crimson Lotus' underground distribution points. Hiroshi and Kenji had been able to infiltrate the facility...but only long enough to ascertain it was yet another decoy front before being overwhelmed. The gangster who'd made the intro was yet another link in Rei's ever-expanding chain of misdirection tactics.

Hence their extreme situation now, staring down the only potential thread of truth they'd been able to pry loose - and quickly running out of time before the Yakuza bosses realized one of their foot soldiers was missing. A hard turn had to be taken to get results before the window slammed shut.

Nodding tersely at Kenji, Hiroshi strode forward and crouched to meet their prisoner's swollen gaze levelly. The gangster's eyes slitted open with effort, throat working as he took in Hiroshi's impassive mask.

"W-who....?"

The first blow came without warning, Kenji's titanium knuckledusters cracking across the mobster's jaw with brutal force. Teeth sprayed along with a garbled shout of shock and pain.

"We'll ask the questions," Kenji stated coldly. "And just to make sure we have your full cooperation going forward..."

The hacker's free hand extended, and with a flick of a control stud, his signature micro-drones slithered free of their casings. Thumbnail-sized but horrifically potent, the glittering killers hovered in a menacing cloud around the prisoner's face - ominous metal wings buzzing with static charge.

Wide eyes darting between them frantically, the Yakuza enforcer began thrashing anew, every breath wheezing wet panic. "Wait... waitwaitwait! I'll talk, I'll tell you everything, just don't-"

Another sharp crunch of knuckles on cartilage cut him off with a garbled scream as bone shattered.

"Save your begging," Kenji said dispassionately. "You'll talk regardless. The question is how much you want to suffer before we get the intel we need."

With a final terrified look at the hovering drones, the gangster slumped back in defeat, eyes squeezing shut. After a moment, he gave a tiny, choked nod.

Rising to his feet, Hiroshi regarded the now-compliant henchman with a detached mask. Deep down, he almost pitied the punk for being a lamb led to slaughter. But that same well of empathy also hardened his resolve - because finding the answers they sought was quite literally a matter of life or death on a much grander scale.

"Make it easier on yourself and cooperate," he said impassively. "We can spare your worthless hide only so much restraint before ramping up our interrogation to the more...advanced techniques."

At that, the prisoner's breath hitched noticeably. His one remaining eye cracked open a slit, studying Hiroshi warily.

"A-advanced...?" His tongue peeked out to wet cracked lips nervously. "Like... like what exactly?"

Hiroshi simply looked at him in cold silence. Let the lowlife's imagination spin out worst-case scenarios of the unspeakable agony that could await him. All it required was the right trigger phrase or visual cue to Kenji, and his darkest fever dream imaginings would manifest as horrific reality.

After several tense heartbeats ticking by, the Yakuza finally sucked in a ragged breath and ducked his chin in a tiny nod of surrender.

"Okay...okay, I'll talk. Tell you everything I know, I swear." He offered up a ghastly shattered smile, crooked teeth striped with smoker's yellow. "No need to...advance nothin', I'll lay it all out. Just...just please, no more of this,"

Hiroshi allowed himself a fractional dip of his chin in grim acknowledgment. Behind him, Kenji's sneer was evident in his tone as he leaned in closer, fingers hovering near his control stud ominously.

"Then start unloading the full gospel, punk. On who pulled your strings in the Crimson Lotus and where that rabid dog Rei Akira has her main kennel..."

Because as much as the criminal scum professed cooperation, they both knew better than to trust a single syllable until it was fully extracted. With the surgical precision of grim artists - and a willingness to mutilate their canvas as needed to produce the desired masterwork.

For at long last, they'd reached the precipice of unleashing the full depths of their ruthlessness. All in pursuit of the truth that could lead them straight into Rei Akira's darkest sanctum... Or confirm their absolute defeat at the hands of her sadistic grand deceptions.

Exhausted and filthy as he was, the Yakuza henchman seemed to recognize the barely-checked savagery in their eyes. He swallowed hard, perhaps realizing there were indeed worse fates than even drawing his last breath under torture tonight.

After a pregnant pause, he took a deep, fortifying breath and began unburdening his blackened soul of every salacious detail regarding the Crimson Lotus he could recall. With every passing minute, new layers of Rei's convoluted schemes and rabbit holes peeled away, yielding more hints at the true extent of her grand designs against them...and all of Tokyo.

By the time the pitifully shattered gangster wheezed his final revelations - pausing only to cough up flecks of lung-tinged spittle - a grim new clarity had hardened in Hiroshi and Kenji's eyes alike. For all the misdirection and pain endured, finally they had credible illumination of the path to the heart of Rei Akira's serpentine labyrinth.

The only question remaining was whether this was the ultimate disclosure they sought...or merely another elaborate trap baited to lure them ever further down the spiral. One could never underestimate the depth of Rei's deceptions, after all.

When Kenji reached out wordlessly to staunch the flow of fresh gore from the prisoner's split lips, Hiroshi stopped his partner's hand with a terse shake of his head. "I think our friend here has shared every nightmare he's privy to about the Crimson Lotus' operations. Any further effort would only yield more suffering, not answers."

The borderline regretful look flickering across Kenji's expression proved it wasn't just an act of mercy, however. Neither of them wanted to tempt probing too far from their captive, risking pushing him past the threshold of permanent damage from which not even a broken mind could recover. And with that would vanish any lucid remnants of potential leads they'd gleaned from his compulsory confessions tonight.

While the information purged under duress might ultimately guide them into the viper's nest itself, a thin veneer of honor still prompted them to leave the hollowed husk breathing. Even a scrap of professional integrity had its limits when dealing with a worm who'd been so eager to slither under Rei's venomous heel.

For the moment, it would have to be enough to prepare themselves for the next slithering segment of this serpentine trail. The point where it inevitably delivered them straight into the coiled embrace of their most lethal adversary yet – and her deadliest fanged ambush of all.

6

A Tightening Vice

The interrogation had been a grim necessity, but Hiroshi couldn't deny a sense of relief once their battered captive finally broke down and began spilling everything he knew about Rei Akira's operations. Maybe now, at long last, they'd have the real intel needed to cut through her labyrinth of deceptions.

Kenji wasted no time cross-checking and triangulating the Yakuza gangster's confessions against all their prior data. While the hardened criminal underbelly always came with a heavy coating of lies and exaggerations, certain pivotal pieces began sliding into place. Coded communications, underground transit routes, shadow facilitation networks...

"I'll be damned," the hacker muttered, dragging a hand back through his disheveled hair. "This all tracks with some of the deeper rabbit holes I've tentatively mapped but never confirmed."

Hiroshi frowned, studying the snarled geographic overlays and transcribed audio logs Kenji was piecing together. "Meaning we've got a legitimate chance at pinpointing Rei's central staging area? Her command bunker?"

"More than that." Kenji shot him a look equal parts grim and electrified. "I'm seeing hints at potential locations for her main research and development hub too. Places she's been cooking up her next-gen technology completely off the grid."

That caught Hiroshi's attention in a way few other things could. He knew all too well just how formidable Rei Akira's illicit arms manufacturing capabilities already were. The thought of her cultivating an entire new generation of bleeding-edge weapons tech...It didn't bear dwelling on the catastrophic damage that could result if such a technological force was turned against the world at large. They had to shut her down by any means necessary.

"Okay, consolidate everything we've got into your most high-confidence assessments," Hiroshi said, mind already racing with tactical scenarios to infiltrate and neutralize the most likely candidates. "I'll start plotting out infiltration vectors and contingencies. We take the fight to her this time before she can spring another trap."

Kenji's mouth set in a grim line, but he nodded once in understanding before turning back to his screens with renewed intensity. For all his general reluctance, he knew as well as Hiroshi that the time for covert games of cat-and-mouse had officially run out. This was their chance to cut the head off the serpent before its victims multiplied into the millions.

Over the next several hours, the small team committed entirely to the new mission parameters of ultimate penetration and shutdown. Kenji spearheaded the analytic offensives, scouring every scrap of data for potential final locations. While Hiroshi forged the armored point of the spear itself, marshaling both physical and cyber weaponry to deploy at a moment's notice.

By the time they had consolidated high-probability targets and finalized planning, a palpable sense of tension gripped the close quarters like a tightening vice. After weeks of maddeningly twisting trails and near-disastrous pitfalls, they'd reached the precipice of head-to-head confrontation with their deadliest quarry, Rei Akira - criminal queen, industrial arms magnate, and utterly remorseless grand mastermind of carnage. To even reach this phase of planning a definitive strike against the heart of her empire felt almost...inevitable. As if the entire sordid saga of pursuit and deception had been herding them toward this single decisive moment of truth.

The question was whether this represented the true coup de grace, or simply the latest convoluted feint in Rei's sadistic brainteaser of a master game.

"We all geared up and ready to roll?" Hiroshi's voice cut the tension like a razor as he double-checked his gear with sharp efficiency. "This is it, partner...our one shot at bringing this whole nightmare firmly to an end."

From behind his command console, Kenji gave a tight nod, eyes narrowed as he communicated brisk final instructions into his comm unit. "All support uplinks are spooled and burning. Ready to hack, spoof, and fry anything with an active circuit in an instant."

"Good." Hiroshi chambered a round in the massive sidearm he'd liberated from one of Rei's elite henchmen during an earlier op. The heavily modded automatic was more of a crew-served personal cannon than a pistol, but its sheer brute force would be invaluable in the coming storm. "Because if my read of this intel is right...we're gonna need every single edge we can muster when we kick Rei's front door down on top of her."

At that, Kenji couldn't quite hide a reflexive wince. For all his skill and experience, the thought of brute-force frontal assaults against unknown defensive arrays clearly didn't rest easily with him. "And you're sure about the primaries? Because I get the feeling a head-on breach would be right up that sicko's alley for baiting a trap..."

Hiroshi's eyes remained locked on his with unblinking intensity. "A feint, a gambit, or an actual chance to strike at the heart of her operations...only one way to find out." He hefted his sidearm meaningfully. "By hitting her where she lives and not pulling our punches for a second."

Because hesitation or half-measures would get them both killed in an instant by the likes of Rei Akira. To even reach this far necessitated wielding the same pitiless drive and full-purge mentality as their monstrous adversary herself.

At last, Kenji simply gave a sharp nod of understanding, squaring his shoulders as the weight of the moment settled upon them.

"Okay then. Let's do this, partner." His lips quirked in a bitter smile utterly devoid of humor. "No more chasing shadows and double-blinds after tonight. Time to light this whole damn maze on fire once and for all."

Without another word, he powered up his offensive cyberdeck suites to full potency, arming every single hardline infiltrator and militant virus package in his arsenal. Miniature fleets of hunter-killer microdrones began spooling up their plasma disruptors and EMP cannons in preparation for deployment.

Taking one last look around their makeshift staging area, Hiroshi felt the world compress to this single pinpoint of resolution. Weeks of sacrifice, violence, and dizzying deception to run their nemesis to ground. It all came down to this - the breach and entry operation that would cap off the mission one way or another.

With a steadying exhale, he armed the fail-safe detonator sewn into his jacket lining. A single press would trigger munitions-grade-shaped charges to vaporize every last shred of intel regarding their pursuit of Rei Akira. Leaving her precious criminal enterprise crippled...but with all their remaining comrades in the dark about her vast shadow war.

It was a calculated risk, but one that had to be embraced without reservation for even a chance at mission success. For weeks now, Rei had dominated them with psychological manipulation and misdirection.

But tonight, the tables were finally, ruthlessly turned. Now it fell to Hiroshi and Kenji to rewrite the rules entirely as they plunged straight into the dragon's den without quarter.

This was no longer a game of cunning hunting tactics or defensive contingencies. From this point forward, only a single ethos applied as they made their final push.

They had been the hunters. They had been the prey.

Tonight, they became the extinction itself. And any who stood in their path would simply cease to exist at all.

The coordinates Kenji's analysis had pinpointed represented one of the city's oldest industrial areas - an overgrown, semi-abandoned manufacturing zone slowly being swallowed by Tokyo's ever-encroaching suburban sprawl. Row after row of rusting factory buildings and weed-choked parking lots made for a perfect clandestine stronghold, provided one knew the exact entry vectors.

Which was where their excruciating intel-gathering had finally paid off in spades. Between the data mined from Rei's computer networks and the backtracked shipment logs forcibly extracted from her henchmen, they'd been able to triangulate the pivotal site to within a few square blocks.

Now came the hard part - penetrating whatever deadly gauntlet of externalized defenses and interior countermeasures the yakuza queen had emplaced around her inner sanctum.

"Talk to me about outer perimeter security," Hiroshi muttered under his breath as they went firm for a final observation. Pulling a compact spycam rig from his vest, he began discreetly snapping high-res overheads of the target zone from their concealed vantage point.

"Multiple layers of sensor sweeps and counter-surveillance," Kenji replied briefly, eyes locked on his data pad as he toggled through a dizzying array of tactical assessments. "IR motion trackers, millimeter wave grids, maybe even ground-penetrating radar if this witch splurged on the excessive countermeasures again."

"In other words, no chance of just ghosting our way inside undetected," Hiroshi concluded grimly.

"Not unless you know someone with a fully accredited id-spoofed maintenance crew and a shielded ground transit vehicle." A considering pause as new intel overlays filtered across Kenji's screen. "...which doesn't seem to be an impossibility here, surprisingly. There's existing subway utility tunnels that could theoretically get us within a few hundred yards if our cloaking tech holds up."

As Kenji showed him the schematics, Hiroshi frowned. Getting that close to the outer perimeter would be risky enough on its own. But then having to find a breach point and penetrate whatever inner defensive layers Rei no doubt had waiting...

"Could be walking straight into another elaborate trap," the agent muttered, more thinking out loud than voicing actual doubt. At this juncture, he'd made peace with the reality that his showdown with Akira might very well be unfolding according to some magnificent script she'd laid out from the beginning. Provided their determination and tactical understanding proved sharper than her narrative framework, it might not matter in the end.

To finally have the chance at closing with the viper directly, at last…that alone was worth hazarding any final bite from her fangs.

"That's always the risk, isn't it?" Kenji pointed out with a shrug. "Hell, this whole op could theoretically have been an insanely elaborate feint to lure us into her snare. But we still have to take the shot while we can, right?"

Hiroshi's mouth tightened fractionally. "Damn right we do." His eyes narrowed as he took one more look at the innocuous-seeming compound holding such lethal secrets. "Get your crew van IDs spoofed and rally the transit tugs. This is our chance to cut the head off the snake once and for all."

"Roger that, partner." With a few swift keystrokes, Kenji channeled his avatar into Rei's private networks, spinning an intricate web of electronic camouflage and misdirection around their physical insertion plan. "Penetration raid on the Crimson Queen's personal hive in ten minutes."

There wasn't even a shred of hesitation or doubt in the hacker's tone - just the same cold resolution they'd both been cultivating for months as they gutted their way ever closer to this flashpoint confrontation.

The time for hedging and cautious gambits had finally expired. Either they seized this singular chance at definitive impact on their target…or they would be consumed along with so many others who'd blundered into Rei Akira's lethal web and never resurfaced.

Ten minutes later, their appropriated maintenance convoy rolled up to the innocuous service entrance, their cloned ID-packages having bypassed all external scrutiny flawlessly. Now came the real test - whether they'd accurately gamed out the interior countermeasures as well.

"Full checklists confirmed and countermeasures hot," Kenji stated tersely over their secure comms. "All units spinning active jamming, stand by for direct ingress on your mark."

Rather than reply, Hiroshi simply shouldered his way through the crevasse-like tunnel entrance, sidearming his massive automatic as soon as he was past the outer checkpoint. While Kenji and his cyber teams manned the spoofers and code overrides, he and the assault squad would handle any actual hostile contacts with extreme prejudice.

The corridor seemed to stretch endlessly before them into shadows and stale recycled air. But with all their planning and technical advantages, their initial infiltration was almost routine. Too routine...

This meant the lethal surprises would only be triggered once they'd advanced far enough to be separated from any quick exit routes.

"I'm reading heavy-duty access chokes ahead," Kenji's voice warned over the comm, sounding suddenly on edge. "Reinforce bulkheads, screened emplacements...could be that we're about to hit the first in a series of-"

His words choked off in a burst of panic and yelling as an echoing roar exploded through the tunnel system behind them. Hiroshi spun reflexively, only to see their parked convoy they had left for crew van suddenly engulfed in a blinding volatile fireball that swept down the length of the service tunnel in a jet of nuclear fury!

"–traps," Kenji finished unnecessarily, his tone now a study in cold dread. "That blast just took out our exit route...and anyone manning overwatch from the secondary teams..."

Throat tightening, Hiroshi forced the shockwave of screams and chaos into a subdued corner of his consciousness. There could be time to mourn the fallen later. Right now, they had to focus on the imminent fact that whatever they were facing, Rei Akira had known their plan from the beginning...and wanted them precisely where they now found themselves.

With no option but to advance further into her lethal crosshairs or retreat into oblivion itself.

"We're boxed in but alive," he rasped towards Kenji's comm signal amid the smoke and groaning metal. "You still have control of her internal systems?"

"For the moment," the reply came back strained. "But that massive shockwave's gonna start scattering my overrides any second now. Once it does, all her physical countermeasures revert to standing lethal codes on us..."

"Copy that." Hiroshi paused to rack the slide of his cannon pistol decisively. "Then we've got one narrow window to turn this around and hit Rei directly before everything comes crashing down around our ears."

No response, save the barest of percussive nods across his HUD indicator. Of course Kenji understood the tactical situation with the same clarity – they had been sprinting blindly into Rei Akira's endgame from the very beginning...and now found themselves squarely in the serpent's kill zone.

Still, some pivotal survival instinct drove Hiroshi to lash out one final time at the sadistic mistress who'd manipulated them to this point. To gamble every last bit of strength and sanity not in being slain like rats in her maze...but scraping their way through to the inner sanctum and planting their defiance onto her very doorstep.

Here in the belly of her final and most uncompromising trap, the option to blink or flinch had been purged permanently. The only path remaining was to press forward with ruthless ferocity, break through her coils at any cost while they still could, and unleash whatever madness lay waiting on the far side.

"Breach and override procedures," he growled harshly across the team channel. "We're going in hot on your virus deployment count."

His last order before the trap's jaws snapped viciously and closed around them for good.

7

Closing In

The tunnel stretched endlessly before them, fading into shadowy darkness punctuated only by rows of flickering industrial lights. Hiroshi felt sweat beading on his brow as their maintenance convoy trundled forward, the air growing thicker and more oppressive with each rattle of the chassis.

"How much further to the projected breach point?" he murmured over the secure comm channel, fingers instinctively tightening around the grip of his suppressed rifle.

"Just ahead," came Kenji's terse reply from the front cab. "My schematics have us hitting one of the main utility junctions in about three hundred meters. From there, it's half a klick through auxiliary transit tubes to bring us up inside Rei's central compound."

Hiroshi flexed his jaw grimly. Five hundred meters - the last span of tunnel separating them from Rei Akira's bleeding crimson heart itself. Assuming she hadn't already reversed every last shred of the system exploits allowing their infiltration and recoded her inner sanctum for maximum lethality against them.

One way or another, the viper's endgame snare would snap inevitably shut once they committed to breaching that final security perimeter. Hiroshi had made peace with that inevitability during the sleepless nights plotting this desperation assault. Better to force Rei's hand and risk obliteration than cower forever from her darkness.

"Take us in," he rasped out, racking the bolt on his rifle decisively. "No mercy, remember? We don't stop until this syndicate's heart stops beating."

Kenji's laugh was utterly devoid of humor across the comm hiss. "You don't have to sell me on putting this twisted matriarch down, Hiroshi. All part of the game plan since the first piece of gathered intel sparked this whole op."

The utility van slowed fractionally as they neared the first junction lockdown, Kenji performing dizzying trinary pirouettes across coded access points to trick the internal sentries into granting them safe passage further into Rei's web. Hairline fractures in the electronic mirror, impossible to detect through conventional surveillance...but each one potentially destabilizing their cover identities past any hope of retrieval.

It was a high-stakes gamble every bit as perilous as the scorpion's nest they'd willingly flung themselves into midst. But for the chance to sever the Crimson Lotus syndicate's beating black heart with one definitive strike, the both of them would happily wager everything remaining.

The convoy lurched to a ponderous halt as they reached the final security vent leading into the central compound's outer periphery. Several seconds of static-laced silence as Kenji waged arcane cyber warfare against Rei's firewalled safeguards. Then a protracted groan of hydraulics as the massive blast door began retracting onto its track against all murderous algorithmic instincts.

"We're in," the hacker grunted at last, sweat beading on his pallid features from the exertion. "Outer lockdown unsealed, interior schematics exposed. Looks like a straight support shaft puts us up into the secondary sublevel junction..."

Hiroshi grunted in acknowledgment, visibly bracing for anything as the convoy ground its way over the threshold into the unknown pitch of Rei's arachnid lair. Overlaid tactical graphics flickered in the corners of his retinal HUD, ready to hose him with a flood of mission-critical data at the first thermal ping.

Strangely, he found himself hoping for immediate resistance – a hail of defensive countermeasures to shred their deception and force them into unequivocal open battle with the enemy. Better that than to suffocate indefinitely in the python's grip of the Crimson Queen's cryptic schemes.

But apart from the groan of strained metal and their own hammering pulses, there was only an eerie silence reverberating through the tubular access tunnels ushering them deeper towards Rei's inner sanctum. An exhalation of humid air mixed with the taint of technology gone sour.

"Keep those countermeasure spoofers primed," Hiroshi cautioned lowly as the shadowy walls pressed claustrophically inward. "I got a hunch her redaction traps are set to spring once we pass the nexus tertiary – right smack in the killzone's crosshairs."

Kenji's teeth gnawed down on his lower lip in concentration. "Roger that, no joy on the easy evacuatoin route either. If we get pinned down in those echoing corridors, extraction's gonna be a nightmare against direct fire-lines and hard interlocks..."

He didn't have to elaborate on the futility of hoping for rapid exfiltration and retreat once they inevitably triggered the serpent's viciously coiled defensive matrices. Rei wouldn't simply settle for repelling them - she'd use whatever sadistic contingencies she'd seeded to utterly eliminate them within these strangling confines.

No quarter asked for those who dared trespass into the den of her cultured savagery, no mercy granted the trespasser...

Which meant their only paths remaining were success or annihilation.

As if in visceral response, the rhythmic boom of the chassis abruptly faded to a dull whine. In the same instant, Kenji's backlit grimace twisted in renewed desperation. "Aw hell... proximity trigger hit! She's already started recoging all my overrides against primed lethals!"

The convoy jolted sickeningly underfoot as something detonated with an avalanche roar in the tunnel behind them. Before Hiroshi could process what was happening, the shock front slammed into them like a physical fist - pitching the van into a hellish frenzy of shearing metal and screaming fuses!

Everywhere he looked, monitors flashed cascading idents of recognition failure. Their electronic camoflauge had just been obliterated in one single ignition of the viper's searing fang! Strapped into the palsied death throes of their compromised vehicle, Hiroshi could only grit his teeth against the high-pitched whine of flayed circuitry and await the next rippling detonation to complete the kill.

"Systems fried!" Kenji hollered over the chaos, his fingers flying madly across the spasming HUD controls. "But I've still got partial overrides on exterior bulkhead defenses for the next three hundred seconds if I allocate a bypass!"

He didn't have to spell the direness any further. Once Rei's lethally encrypted central security grid finished countering the last traces of Kenji's intrusion codes, they'd be facing a hurricane of autonomic countermeasures at point-blank. Turrets, scans, seeker grenades - all the most demonic defensive technologies known to man or corporation...

Three hundred seconds to commit to their do-or-die gambit against the heart of the Crimson Queen's hive before they drowned in the apocalypse barreling towards them!

Nodding curtly, Hiroshi wrenched his rifle from its buckled traverse rack as their stricken convoy ground to a shuddering halt. He could already taste the scent of battle stoking itself in the confined atmosphere. "Breach and override count it is. Use my fireteam as primary shock-troopers against any direct threat reprisals!"

"Copy that!" Even as klaxons began a maddening dissonance all around them, Kenji was already frantically hijacking what slim advantage remained from Rei's own countermeasure systems. "Got a read on the inner sanctum's geodesics from here! Straight down that maintenance tunnel and breaching hard left after five level drops!"

They'd have to fight every agonizing meter of that hardline advance against the swarming defenses awakening from their slumber all around them. But it was the only way to bring their long shadow war against Rei Akira to its cataclysmic conclusion!

Squaring his stance, Hiroshi unleashed a rattling decompression burst into the twisting service corridors before them. Then he triggered his comm with a snarl of implacable resolve:

"All units go red and punch through to the heart of this viper pit! The Crimson Lotus queen doesn't get to claim another night's reign over these streets!"

With that, he plunged headlong into the waiting pandemonium - grenades detonating like hellish suns in every direction as Rei's lethal countermeasures finally ignited to full autonomic fury.

Smoke billowed in acrid clouds as Hiroshi plunged deeper into the serpentine corridor network, rifle blazing defiantly against the torrent of explosive countermeasures detonating all around them. Behind his fireteam, he could hear Kenji's voice barking frantic override commands against the rapidly adapting security matrix.

"Multiple auto-turrets spinning stalker streams from behind!" the hacker's voice crackled over the cacophony of violence. "I've got a thirty-second window to spoof their friend-foe IFF before they lock for slashing fire!"

Sparing a glance over his shoulder, Hiroshi saw the deadly gun drones unfolding from armoured alcoves with lethal precision - their extruded sensor stalks already pivoting to acquire their fleeing signatures with ruby streaks of target painters.

"Smoke 'em!" he snarled into his comm unit, half a second before lobbing a plethora of grenades down the intersecting kill corridor.

The high-explosive grenades detonated in twin blooms of scorching vapors, momentarily smothering the turrets' optics in a shroud of dense particulates. But it wouldn't blind them for long, not against their thermal imaging reserves and motion tracker algorithms.

As if to punctuate that fact, a staccato burst of armor-piercing shards raked through the smoke, gnawing chunks from the tunnel's structural bracings mere feet from where Hiroshi's team was bounding in desperation retreat. The pursuing storm of autofire spun ever closer behind them, calibrating through the interference with each passing nanosecond.

"Got the spoofer spliced!" Kenji yelled in grim satisfaction, his madly scrolling hack codes having temporarily overridden the turrets' identification matrices. "They're flagging us as blue now - you should have...aw crap, thirty seconds tops before she cycles a purge lockout!"

Even their respite would be fractional at best against Rei's increasingly adaptive countermeasures. But fractal windows were all they could hope to scavenge during this panicked headlong rush towards the inner sanctum.

If they managed it at all... The raging cacophony of detonations and autonomous weapon struggles echoed louder ahead of them, the closer they neared their ultimate destination.

"Keep pushing," Hiroshi bellowed to his team in between lucid gasps. "We stall out here and all our stacked bones get left behind in this hellpit!"

Not that the prospect of Rei Akira's subterranean incinerator awaiting them deeper inside was any more inspiring as a final recourse. But better a last stand against the viper itself than choking on her coils while cowering halfway between sanctuary and the abyss.

Another frenzied exertion brought them skidding around a fractal corner, into an open hexagonal chamber strewn with the smoldering wreckage of previous intruders' demise. Instantly, the overhead braziers ignited, bathing the entire space in hellish crimson illumination - as scything bursts of liquid munitions stitched blazing impact craters all around them.

"Down!" Hiroshi screamed, hitting the deck in the same desperate slide as the rest of his fireteam. Above them, a flechette barrage hammered home like shrieking metal rain, ripping apart anything left standing.

"Working on those too!" came Kenji's barked update from

somewhere within the reverberating melee. "But her recourse lockouts are cycling faster each time, adaptive layers primed to reinitialize!"

Translation - with every countermeasure spoofing attempt, Rei's central AI was deftly adjusting code banks to prioritize that specific infiltration exploit out of their arsenal. What minimal advantage they'd gained these past few desperate minutes wouldn't last...

With a defiant growl, Hiroshi twisted onto his back and started battling the interlocked turret streams with sweeping blasts of his own. They were losing ground with every ticking second, pinned in the cyclone's eye of this insane security overlapping - but he'd be damned if they receded a single centimeter further from their objective

"Push through that choke point!" he roared over the din, gesturing with the barrel of his smoldering rifle towards the far egress shuttering wildly beneath the lethal crossfire storm. "We're not dying here, not before we get to the witch that set this whole mad game in motion!"

Whether or not his fire team obeyed in that moment blurred into irrelevance as the battle turned to a full-fledged melee of motion and violence. Hiroshi's rifle emptied itself in a stream of ricocheting pain until he was forced to abandon the overheated chassis - then it was simply his bare fists against whatever mechanized hostiles were within reach.

At some point, he wrenched an entire gun turret from its swivelling mooring and began using the entire apparatus as a brutal bludgeon against its own automated kin. Steel shrieked like a banshee as he brought the makeshift maul down again and again, smashing them apart in percussive eruptions of debris and ozone.

His scream of defiance became a snarling battle cry echoing through every corridor of Rei's subterranean killing maze - a focused distillation of every hope, atrocity and sacrifice that had guided him to this climactic confrontation.

Until at last, through a red mist of exhaustion, exsanguination, and seared electronics, he glimpsed open space beyond the crossfire nexus. Not a clear avenue by any stretch - just a momentary recess and gasping reprieve before the next erupting storm of countermeasures inevitably lashed out from whatever lurked past this charnel threshold.

But it was enough to trigger one last, wrenched reserve of momentum from his battered form. With a bestial roar, Hiroshi vaulted the wreckage and plunged through the swirling smoke, whatever fragments of his team remained bounding in desperate pursuit on his heels.

They spilled out onto some sort of suspended network access platform overlooking an industrial chasm below. For a fractured heartbeat of respite, Hiroshi allowed himself to collapse on all fours and retch up the noxious fumes boiling within his lungs.

But the keening shriek of proximity sensors swiftly reminded him that there would be no quarter here, no true safe harbor to tend to their wounds. Rei's own personal sentries and inner defensive mandates were already spiraling in around them with undiminished ferocity!

"Okay," Kenji gasped out as he lurched to an unsteady combat crouch beside Hiroshi. The hacker's youthful features were ravaged with equal measure of blood, ash, and naked dread - as if he already knew they'd plunged directly into the heart of the most unforgiving hell imagined. "Any...any bright idea what we do next before they burn us to cinders from every direction?"

All around them, Hiroshi could already see the outlines of

reinforced bulwarks and chokepoints where legions of security drones were rapidly assembling. The cyclonic maelstrom of destruction they'd endured merely to reach this pivotal junction now paled in the face of what was about to detonate point-blank across their positions.

But for all his desperation, some deeper reservoir of cold determination persisted in Hiroshi's core. Some unwavering faith that the only path now remained to seize and then force this climactic confrontation to its inexorable conclusion...regardless of how much blood and ruin were required to clear the killing-ground beforehand.

"Press on," he rasped out savagely, the words scraping from his throat with a lifetime's bitter gravitas. "We go for the heart - for HER! Let her sentinels batter us all the way to her final sanctum if they dare!"

His gaze met Kenji's then without flinching. "No retreat now. No turning back until the Crimson Queen's reign burns to ash at our feet. Time to see who truly thrives from the scorched remains of midnight Tokyo..."

8

Rei Akira

The platform shuddered violently as a fresh salvo of armor-piercing rounds chewed into its buckled surface mere inches from where Hiroshi was braced. Beside him, Kenji flinched involuntarily at the proximity of those whip-crack detonations.

"They've got hard-locks triangulating our position!" the hacker shouted over the escalating chaos, his slim hands dancing urgently across the holographic screens of his wrist-mounted infiltrator rig. "Rei's core security architecture is purging every last remnant of my overrides now!"

Which meant any slim technological edge they'd leveraged on this desperation push was about to be nullified in one apocalyptic stroke. Within seconds, the full autonomous force of the Crimson Queen's lethal citadel would be unleashed against them uninhibited - and there would be no quarter given or mercy granted.

Hiroshi's lips peeled back in a savage snarl of defiance as he pivoted onto a knee and started snapping off aimed bursts toward the nearest converging turret nests. Each report of his sidearm cannon punched a new smoking crater from whatever armored bulwark the opposing hostiles had assembled themselves behind.

"Then quit fighting her digital shadow war and let me take point blasting our way through!" he bellowed at Kenji in between the staccato thunderclaps. "We're not going to logic-job ourselves past her inner sanctum! We'll have to cleave our own path straight through, guns blazing!"

A heartbeat's hesitation from the hacker, as if he could scarcely process this mad desperation gambit from his more level-headed partner. But Hiroshi could already see the cold resignation calcifying behind Kenji's eyes in the same instant. Just as it had in his own soul several fire-swept battlezones ago.

There came a climactic juncture on every shadow op where the folly of further subterfuge had to be accepted - and nothing remained except the willingness to escalate onto a more primal plane of unrestrained violence in pursuit of their objective. To either crush through to their target with unwavering ferocity...or be utterly consumed by the flames of their own arrogance.

"Fine!" Kenji spat out a mouthful of copper onto the platform deck. "I'll stick to cycling refresh waves against her firewalls, keep them as unstable as possible for however long we can hold out! But you'd better be the best samurai with that cannon or this just turned into our last stand!"

The words had scarcely solidified in the air before the storm descended upon them with full fury! Hiroshi instinctively flung himself behind a half-melted spar of bulkhead as the first hurricane blasts chewed into their position like a gargantuan serrated buzzsaw seeking to rend them limb from limb.

But rather than cower or go defensive against this abhorrent onslaught, he found himself charging back towards the lip of their exposed vantage with a primal roar of indignation -

answering the soulless weaponized thunderheads with blazing volleys of his own high-explosive contempt!

To either side of him, whatever remnants of his fireteam had survived this far began responding in kind with a cacophony of supportive gunfire. Whether they were fighting to breach towards Rei or merely battling for one more futile moment of survival now blurred into irrelevance.

Hiroshi had crossed that pivotal gap separating focused strategy from outright feral determination long ago during the tunnels' choking cataclysms. Now it all distilled to that singular imperative: unleashing maximum lethality until nothing remained except him or the target.

He was already halfway to the far entrenchment blasting a raging corridor through its lines before he'd even processed what was happening! Through smoke and high explosive shrapnel spume, Hiroshi bored relentlessly onward like a human battering ram - letting out all the wrath that had distilled over a lifetime upon the hapless drones fruitlessly attempting to repel his inexorable advance.

At one point he glimpsed a morbid vision of limbs carved from pillars of ruby lasefire - but couldn't tell if they were his own or some immolating henchman of Rei's. All that mattered was the relentless drumbeat explosions rocking closer towards the central citadel.

Soon he wasn't even truly aiming his cannon anymore, just blasting anarchic fusillades blindly from the hip into whatever fleeting thermal silhouettes his optics glimpsed through the charcoal stormfront. The air reeked of partially burnt flesh and acrid smoke...some of it no doubt his own cauterized wounds.

How many more exultations he must unleash into that immersive madness before feeling the slick impact of bulkhead plating against his back was impossible to gauge. What Hiroshi did know was the sudden sickening recognition that he now had line of sight on Rei Akira's inner sanctum itself - visible beyond a final choking gauntlet of intersecting shredder streams boxed in around its thresholds!

The heart of the Crimson Viper's corruption, a festering crimson nerve-bundle of reinforced portals and sensor hubs... pulsing and breathing with a subterranean cadence all its own amid the Wagnerian bombast of their brutal encroachment. The seat of the diabolical power poised to strangle all of Tokyo into a single choking coil of vice.

And between them and whatever sadistic horrors lurked waiting beyond those chilling portals stood only the remorseless storm of raging gun killers they'd already weathered to reach this pivotal threshold. Just one more focused battering push through the crossfire - one final exertion of defiance powerful enough to annihilate all in its path!

Abruptly, Hiroshi felt the weight of Kenji's restraining grip on his shoulder, the hacker's desperate voice gurgling in his ear. "Steady, steady! We have to time this last push perfectly! If you go against that overlapping crossfire, you'll be spattered and pasted before you cross the..."

But the rest of his urgent counsel dissolved into silence as Hiroshi felt a swell of bloodthirsty clarity crest within his soul. His friend was right - any normal reckless assault into that thundering hellstorm would only see them systematically dismembered and slaughtered before ever breaching the inner sanctum itself.

But there were other paths still remaining than direct frontal brutality.

Pivoting with an almost passive sense of purpose, Hiroshi

brought his cannon around in one smooth motion to annihilate the overhead pipchase access running parallel to their position. The pillars surrounding him detonated through the superstructure like a thundering line of shaped charges - silhouetting him in a haze of high explosive contrails as the ceiling collapsed in a shrieking rain of twisted girders and debris!

Even as the shock impact bowled him back onto his shoulders, Hiroshi calmly cleared the slide of his sidearm. Then he simply unleashed one measured pistol blast upwards into the rupturing overhead...

...and a thundering avalanche of oblivion came cascading down all around them!

His last conscious memory from that debatably judicious rain of collapsing metal, smoke, and fire was a silent prayer to whatever fates watched over such madness - that they'd miscalculated just enough chaos in their wake to find providence punching through into Rei Akira's sanctum on the far side.

Then all faded to darkness and ruin.

Consciousness slowly filtered back in with the taste of smoke and pulverized concrete dust coating Hiroshi's tongue. His body felt as if it had been passed through a crude human blast furnace. Several agonizing minutes passed before he could muster the strength to open his scorched eyelids.

What awaited his vision should have inspired nothing but stark terror - the towering wreckage-strewn hallmark of complete structural upheaval and smothering ruin in all directions. Were it not for the singular crimson neon lumen piercing through the debris-choked haze like a baleful eye.

A beckoning gateway to some deeper inner realm awaiting them...the final challenge for any who dared pierce through to the black heart of the Crimson Lotus itself.

Every neuron screamed for respite, but the secret operative knew better than to surrender here on the precipice of where many lesser warriors would have long since faltered. Not when he was so achingly close to the bleeding source of the corruption poisoning his city.

Movement flickered in the periphery of the debris field – the unmistakable silhouette of Kenji digging himself out from under a slab of sheared bulkhead. The hacker's face was a mask of stunned disbelief and pain, but he was still breathed defiance.

"You...crazy...son of a...!" Kenji started to rasp out between bloody coughs, only to choke up another stream of viscera that could have been from internal trauma.

Spitting out a mouthful of his own fouled phlegm, Hiroshi merely gestured with his chin towards the gore-slicked path they'd torn open before them. "Quit belly-aching and check your firewalls," he growled, the words slurring around his swollen tongue. "We've got maybe one shredded minute to hit that entry point before her reactivated sentries realize we're still moving!"

As if in punctuation, a series of proximity blasts detonated somewhere deeper inside the citadel's violated center works. An ominous prelude of the closing countermeasures already stirring to remake this breach into their inescapable tomb. They'd punched through, but now the true endgame was rapidly coiling around them with ultimate finality.

But such was the only path left for those willing to face the midnight shroud of Tokyo's underworld in its most maleficent aspect. A gauntlet of flame and furious determination until the final confrontation itself. Anything less would leave the serpent's coils left to inexorably tighten around all they cherished until the last glimmer of light was strangled

"T-Trying..." Kenji managed to extract his comms unit from the wreckage pinning him in place. The holographic projection flickered with static but remained operational as he began cycling fresh system cracks across its encoded overrides.

"Think I can keep our IFFs spoofed for...maybe sixty seconds tops once we cross the threshold. After that it's going to be a straight gunfight slog against whatever auto-butchers she's got waiting on the other side."

Hiroshi nodded grimly, using his last reserves of strength to hoist his rifle back into a combat-ready embrace. The indicator strips along the chassis were glowing a hazardous red, tantalizingly close to venting its entire remaining ordnance payload in one cataclysmic detonation.

He couldn't imagine a more fitting initiator for the finale of this long, bloody trail towards vindication against Rei Akira.

With a groaning of metal and stone, the two warriors levered themselves fully upright and started lurching towards the breach they'd torn into the viper's heart. Every step was sheer agony, a clawing reminder of the sacrifices and unspeakable torments that had led them to this ultimate turning point.

Until at last they stood before the rippling crimson enameled portal beckoning them into Rei's inner sanctum. Beyond those shifting energy fields lay the very source of the sadistic depravity tainting their beloved city. The seed of ultimate corruption from which the Crimson Lotus crime syndicate had metastasized into a strangling shroud no one else could defeat.

"She'll be waiting for us," Hiroshi murmured, steadying his rifle's aim on the shifting threshold. Even now, his combat vision analyzer flickered ominous warnings of countermeasure potentials lying in anticipation on the other side. "Probably some twisted vanity display intended to unhinge us at the last moment. Stay frigid."

Kenji flashed a mirthless grin, his teeth stained pink from internal hemorrhaging. "Always focused on the mission outcomes, no matter how ugly the process. You'd make one hell of a Bushido instructor, Hiroshi."

There was no further need for banter or acknowledgment between the two warriors. With a subtle nod of understanding, Kenji triggered the final override pulse allowing them ingress - while Hiroshi simultaneously depressed the stud that vented his rifle's entire energized payload as a blistering projectile lance of electromagnetic death!

They surged through the aperture as one - a whirlwind of gunfire, ordnance detonation, and primal defiance that swept aside the last vestiges of physical resistance barring their path. Only to sweep up short at the spectacle awaiting them on the far side...

Rei Akira's lair was easily the size of a small pantheon, reinforced against even the most focused orbital bombardment. Suspended in the epicenter of its vaulted amphitheater, like some sort of empress overseeing the pageantry of death, was an enormous spherical regeneration tank filled with sloshing crimson nutrient fluid.

And floating serenely in stasis at the heart of its pulsing, umbilical cradle was some horrific human-hybrid mutation...its skin the colour of aged damask and veined with an insectoid carapace latticework spiraling from a central orb containing the deformed facial features of a once-beautiful woman twisted into a demonic rictus.

The sight was so revolting yet innately compelling in its blasphemous splendor that it took Hiroshi several distracted seconds to process the additional figures standing in attendance before the grotesque spectacle. Crimson-garbed and enrobed elite guards whose bionic faceplates whisked open in the instant they detected his and Kenji's combative intrusion.

In the heartbeat before the first knives and explosive flechettes slashed out from their defensive rings, Hiroshi saw one final damning flicker of comprehension slither across Rei's lipless maw - the vague impression of satisfaction, as if everything had unfolded according to some elaborate baroque masterplan from the very beginning.

Then the chilling laughter began, and their desperate gambit detonated into its ultimate conflagration!

The laughter reverberated through the vaulted chamber like the demented peals of a cracked bell - inhuman in its cadence, devoid of any warmth or sanity. Hiroshi felt his gut clench as the sound washed over him, every tactical instinct screaming that this entire scenario had been meticulously ornamented merely for their arrival.

Rei Akira's personal guard began to advance, their armored boots ringing across the obsidian floor tiles with implacable precision. Hiroshi swung his rifle towards them, but a subtle gesture from the mutated crimson figure suspended in the vitric regeneration tank froze them in place.

"Welcome, my determined architect of conflict," a warped voice slithered from the central orb containing Rei's twisted facial features. "I confess, part of me wondered if your relentless persistence would truly manage to penetrate this far into the sanctum sanctorum without being utterly unmade."

Beside him, Hiroshi felt Kenji tense like a coiled serpent ready to strike at the first provocation. But he held up a restraining hand, his own gaze remaining locked on the grotesque spectacle awaiting them. After everything, he would not allow himself to be so easily unbalanced or wrongfooted.

"I take it the freak show genetic modifications are intended to represent the bloated decadence and corruption at the heart of your criminal empire?" he called out in a tone of studied neutrality. "Or just the literal outcome of bathing yourself in illicit riches and commodities while countless innocents suffered for your indulgences?"

The crimson figure regarded him impassively for a long moment. Then its deformed mouth parted in a disturbingly delighted grin, fanged and glistening with some dark ichor.

"Such...quaint preconceptions about mortal aspiration and what separates the exceptional existence from the dull herd masses," she purred in a voice like sugared toxins. "You'd hardly credit the truth - that the sublime superiority you bear witness to here was the ultimate destination driving me from the beginning, rather than some twisted side-effect of insatiable vice."

Hiroshi's eyes narrowed fractionally. "Enlighten me then. What plane of perfected being could you have possibly pursued that concluded in...that revolting embrace?"

He gestured towards the tubes and umbilici interfacing with the mutated form's flayed anatomy. Revulsion lurked behind his neutral mask, struggling to stay contained. But he refused to allow even a hint of that soul-sickness to bleed through into his demeanor where Rei could taste it.

Her chuckle this time was decidedly toying as if recognizing the deliberate stimulation he was goading her towards. "Just as your narrow breed always assumed the subtle higher mysteries lay solely within your stunted province, detective. That all answers could be grasped and categorized according to your pitiful datastreams of ethics and social constraints."

One of her bio-armored hands drifted out in an idle, beckoning gesture that made Hiroshi's skin want to evacuate his body. "But what if I revealed the truth to you? That for all your prideful self-aggrandizing beliefs about order and the rule of law...in truth, the entire civilized construct you people base your existence upon merely an intricate canvas for a far greater overriding work to be woven into place unseen?"

Hiroshi felt a crawl of ice trickle along his synapses at the mad profundity she was presenting. As if being granted a sickening glimpse into an eldritch reality far too vast and alien for mortal minds to fully apprehend without succumbing to instantaneous madness.

"You're talking about achieving some level of...ascendance," he said, a cold edge creeping into his voice now. Beside him, he could sense Kenji subtly recalibrating his aim towards the pulsing crimson sphere, finger tightening on the trigger guard. "A complete transcendence beyond the human condition as we understand it into a new holistic sublime."

Another fanged smile - this one tinged with the barest frisson of respect, as if he'd grasped more from her ramblings than even she'd expected. "Quite, detective. Once the final ritual triggers are enacted, this ravaged husk I retained for base utilities will at last be permitted to discard its frail encumbrances and soar to greet its apotheosis among the grand unified helices of cosmic infinitum."

The figure began to twist in an obscene pantomime against the regenerative fluids suspending it. Hiroshi felt gorge rising in the back of his throat at the organic sounds of flesh stretching and peristaltic contractions.

"In joining with the higher celestial paradigms, all Earthly concerns shall become as less than motes to me - pain, anguish, rot and transgression transfigured into instruments for seeding the universal manifestation down whichever fertile crucibles will permit the code-keys to take root most expediently."

For one primal instant, Hiroshi was gripped by the insane compulsion to simply empty his entire magazine into the blasphemous figure, no matter what defenses stood arrayed between it and him. Some deep-seated part of his psyche recoiled with visceral revulsion at the very notion of such a sentient abomination being permitted to transcend beyond any conception of being that could be perceived as remotely human.

But then the towering serenity with which Rei floated encapsulated within her protective womb struck him with crystal clarity. Whatever reality she believed herself to be embracing was so far beyond normal reckoning that she'd already achieved a kind of twisted serenity about the final steps remaining on her path.

And that realization promptly extinguished whatever bloodlust had flared up in his soul. Because as fundamentally despicable and wrong as her transformation was on every possible level, it also robbed Rei Akira of the ability to feel vindicated or sated by its completion through any ordinary means.

For all her professed arrogance and egotism, ultimately her crusade to achieve personal apotheosis would see her become not a god among mortals...but rather a half-life celestial entity no longer able to take any real pleasure or pride in the depravities she'd once reveled in orchestrating across the meanstreets of Tokyo.

A hollow existence devoid of further self-actualization and forever marooned outside the universal continuum she'd come to disdain with such violent fervor. All for the sake of a grand unified delusion built upon unfathomable layers of subjective lies.

Hiroshi almost pitied the depths the fabled Crimson Queen had allowed herself to be led down this lightless path of self-annihilation. But more than that, he felt a steely determination to deny her the refuge from closure represented by whatever delusional visions danced behind her flensed eyes.

He met her burning gaze levelly, the grip on his rifle never wavering. "You arrogant, self-deluded fool," he rasped harshly, allowing his full contempt to bleed through at last. "Did you really believe we came here simply to stop whatever sadistic schemes you had in motion for mortal gain? That was never the mission's prime directive."

One hand closed into a trembling fist against the pommel of his gun-stock, tendons rippling starkly. "We came here to put an end to your reign of terror permanently - not just snip away another ramifying strand of your malignant network. And if necessary, to ensure you can NEVER escape beyond our reach through some farcical ritual of rebirth and forced universal ascendance."

Rei regarded him calmly as he spoke, the expression on what remained of her mouth suggesting neither surprise nor acknowledgment of his passionate speech. As if she'd already known the core of his belief systems would not permit him to stand idly while she completed her transfiguration.

Finally, she sighed in a tired echo of her former self. "Then I'm afraid the two of us are fated to share one final sacrament of apotheosis before our paths eternally diverge, detective."

With that, she arched backwards against the tank's amniotic suspension with a sound like breaking timber. And the rows of bodyguards flanking the platform immediately canted open their sleek armoured cowls in unison - swiveling auto-cannons and smart missile batteries blazing towards the interlopers with apocalyptic intensity!

"Kenji, now!" Hiroshi bellowed, simultaneously releasing whatever last failsafes held his own rifle's reactor burn in check!

The two warriors unleashed their combined arsenals in the same heartbeat, a storm of superheat blastwave and hypersonic munitions detonating across the space in a cyclonic frenzy of unleashed devastation!

Rei Akira's crimson bodyguards were quite literally vaporized where they stood, their armored chestwraps and macrobatteries combusting into shotgun bursts of shrapnel that stitched wildly across the vaulted amphitheater. Walls split apart in geysers of shattered permacrete as thermal blooms seared away every trace of adornment and structural integrity.

Suspended at the roiling vortex of this unleashed inferno, the mutated Rei Akira screamed out a protracted howl of indescribable anguish - her regeneration tank's protective housing spalling away layer by scorched layer until she hung exposed within the kiln-hot fury!

Acting on what could only have been some final, desperate confluence of self-preserving urges, the deformed figure lashed out with withered cybernetic tendrils - each pulsing with devastatingly overcharged plasma discharges capable of searing away any remaining threat with a single grazing impact.

Hiroshi and Kenji were hurled apart, riding out the cyclonic expenditure of hellish energies in midair tumbles that cracked bones and set their battleframes smoldering on impact. For just a heartbeat, Hiroshi thought he glimpsed a towering shadow descending amidst the chaos - a grotesque spectral shape of gnarled fury and retribution manifesting to answer the reverberating scream sounding in his ears.

Then all faded to burnt shadows and the acrid stench of failure's ashes.

He awoke gasping, every nerve ending afire with the aftershocks of the near-terminal detonation. The vaulted amphitheater had become a scorched, debris-choked tomb in the wake of their clash with Rei's mortal contingencies. Nothing remained of her bodyguards or armored sentries save a few smoldering EM ghost prints seared into the floor tiles.

At the epicenter of it all, the vitric regeneration chamber lay in a strewn trail of ruptured components...its central nutrient womb conspicuously vacant of any remnant occupant.

A mournful susurration gradually wormed its way into Hiroshi's battered sensorium - the telltale hiss of vented coolant reservoirs and power distribution nodes beginning to fatally destabilize all around them. Rei's sanctum was quite literally unmade, hemorrhaging its vital autonomic force into a screaming, runaway dissipation vector.

They'd won their confrontation with the Crimson Queen at last, pitting every last reserve of resolve and capability against her mortal contingencies and designs...only to behold their foe retreating beyond their grasp into some higher unknown.

"Kenji..." Hiroshi coughed out weakly, trying but failing to lever himself upright against the wreckage spar pinning his midsection in place. "Did we...?"

"She's gone, partner." The hacker's voice sounded hoarse... strained nearly to the breaking point by what they'd just witnessed unfurling around them. "Pulled some kind of dimensional egress at the peak of her...metamorphosis. I'm not even picking up stray chromo-traces or biometrics anywhere - it's like she atomized herself into complete dissipation."

Silence fell between them as they absorbed the magnitude of being denied even a definitive victory against their greatest adversary. Rei's mocking laughter still seemed to linger in the settling particulate clouds all around them, an auditory phantasm taunting them with the inevitability of whatever transcendent path she now walked.

Hiroshi wasn't sure how long they simply lay there in the umbratic aftermath before his comm-implant crackled to grating life with a new voice override cutting through the static:

"Agent Tanaka, Kenji...this is Field Commander Akiva with Oversight Control. We're reading a catastrophic thermal spike and neutrino flare from within the target's sanctum consistent with extremely energized ordnance detonations. Requesting update on the operation's status..."

Hiroshi closed his eyes, permitting himself a single anguished exhalation. Even though Rei's mortal vessel had been unmade, clearly the full cosmic ramifications were only just beginning...

9

A Vengeful Vow

A new wave on henchmen swarmed into the rubble, and gunfire erupted as they did so. Hiroshi and Kenji dove for cover behind a stack of steel crates. Bullets pinged off the metal as they hunkered down.

"Any bright ideas?" Hiroshi shouted over the chaos.

Kenji's eyes darted around, calculating their next move. "I might be able to trigger an EMP burst from my cyberdeck. It would fry their weapons' electronics."

"Do it!"

Kenji's fingers flew across the keyboard of his wrist-mounted computer. With a determined look, he slammed his fist onto the enter key.

A blinding pulse of electromagnetic energy radiated outwards, washing over the room in a wave of crackling blue light. The henchmen's guns sparked and fizzled, rendered useless by the EMP.

"Now's our chance!" Hiroshi sprang up, pistol raised.

A figure stood impassive, seemingly untouched by the EMP burst. One hand gripped a polished katana blade. "Impressive," a woman's voice sneered. "But I don't need guns to defeat you."

Hiroshi looked back to see Rei seemingly untouched and now stood on the central platform.

Her henchmen rushed forward, drawing blades and pipes and anything they could use as an improvised weapon. Hiroshi opened fire, but they kept coming, batting aside his shots with expert skill.

A thug swung a length of chain at Kenji's head. He ducked at the last instant and the chain clanged off the floor. Whipping out a slender cyberblade from his coat sleeve, Kenji met the next attack head-on in a clash of sparks.

Hiroshi traded blows with three masked henchmen, their blades flashing in the dim light. He blocked a sword strike and pivoted, slamming the butt of his pistol into one thug's face. Another kicked his legs out from under him.

Hitting the ground hard, Hiroshi gasped for breath as a boot stamped down on his wrist. He stared up at the leering face of a hulking brute wielding a machete.

Just as the man raised his blade, a blur of movement streaked past. Kenji's cyberblade swept in a glittering arc, severing the thug's hand in a spray of crimson. He howled in agony, dropping the machete as Kenji danced back, chipped blade extended.

Hiroshi scrambled to his feet and rejoined the fray. Side-by-side, he and Kenji fought with grim determination, slowly cutting down Rei's forces.

But the battle was far from over. Their sleek forms whirled through blades slicing the air as they faced off against Rei herself.

Rei was a phantom, her sword an extension of her body. Each strike was a work of lethal precision and elegance. Hiroshi grunted as her blade nicked his shoulder, drawing a line of red.

"You can't win," Rei hissed, pressing her assault. "My skills are beyond anything you'll ever achieve."

Gritting his teeth, Hiroshi deflected the next flurry of blows and launched a furious counterattack. Kenji joined in, forcing Rei onto the defensive.

Their weapons clashed in a deafening cadence of steel and sparks. Hiroshi's muscles burned with exertion as sweat beaded on his brow. Rei fought with cold, controlled fury, her face an icy mask.

Something whistled past Hiroshi's head. A throwing knife struck Kenji's cyberblade, knocking it from his hand. He cried out, clutching his bleeding palm.

In that split second of distraction, Rei moved with blinding speed. Her katana arced up in a blindingly fast slash.

Searing pain blossomed across Hiroshi's torso as the razor-sharp blade bit deep. He stumbled back, gasping, hand pressed to the gaping wound in his side as blood seeped through his fingers.

"Hiroshi!" Kenji shouted in horror.

Rei stood impassive, flicking Hiroshi's blood from her sword. "Did you really think you could defeat me?" she said with utter contempt. "I am the greatest warrior Tokyo has ever seen."

Hiroshi gritted his teeth against the searing pain, his side slick with blood from Rei's brutal slash. He pressed a hand to the wound, trying to staunch the heavy flow.

Rei simply watched with cold disdain as he struggled to remain standing. "You never had a chance against me. I toyed with you for my own amusement, and now the game is over."

She leveled her crimson-stained katana at his heart. "Any last words?"

Hiroshi's fingers inched towards the grenade on his belt. If he could create enough of a distraction, buy Kenji a few crucial seconds...

Suddenly, a familiar voice rang out from the shadows. "Freeze! This is the TKPD Tactical Response Unit! Drop your weapons immediately!"

Heavily armed officers in riot gear emerged from the darkness, rifles trained on Rei and her remaining henchmen. Kenji stood among them, face pale but determined.

At the forefront was TKPD Captain Itsuko Himura, an old friend and mentor to Hiroshi. Her steely gaze swept the scene as she gripped her shotgun.

"It's over, Akira," Himura stated, jaw set. "Your entire criminal empire is being shut down as we speak. Surrender peacefully, or we will open fire."

A muscle twitched in Rei's cheek as she slowly lowered her sword. "Very well," she said through gritted teeth. "I concede this battle. But make no mistake - the Crimson Lotus will bloom again."

With a sharp nod from the captain, the TKPD officers swarmed forward, slapping high-tech restraints on Rei and her men. Two medics hurried to Hiroshi's side, quickly staunching the wound with a foam sealant.

"Easy there," one of them said gruffly as they eased him onto a stretcher. "You'll be patched up in no time."

Rei fixed him with a venomous look as she was led past in chains. "I'll see you again, Tanaka," she vowed in a low voice. "And when I do, there will be a reckoning."

Kenji moved to Hiroshi's side, favoring his injured hand. "I can't believe that actually worked," he muttered. "Using the interrogation intel to track her lair, then calling in Himura's team for backup."

"It was risky," Hiroshi admitted with a pained grimace. "But at least we finally have Akira contained."

"Yeah, for now..." Kenji watched uncertainly as the TKPD marched their captives away.

Hours later, medics finished treating Hiroshi's wounds in a secluded safehouse while Himura debriefed him on the operation's success.

"We dismantled every known Crimson Lotus base of operations across the city," she reported briskly. "Weapons caches, safehouses, recruitment centers, fronts - all of it. Rei's entire network is in ruins."

Papers detailing the extensive raid covered the table between them. Mug shots of Rei's top lieutenants and corporate moles, maps, financial records all spilled out in a dizzying mass of intel.

"What about their corporate side?" Hiroshi asked. "Akira Cybernetics was a multi-billion yen company."

Himura shook her head grimly. "Not anymore. We've seized all their assets and data, hitting them with enough racketeering charges to put the whole board behind bars for decades."

She pulled out a glossy photograph showing an underground facility swarmed by TKPD teams. Vaults stood open, massive computer banks glowing dimly.

"This was the heart of their operation - an illegal cybernetics lab buried beneath Akira Corp HQ. They were manufacturing highly illegal tech and next-gen cyber-implants, all under everyone's noses."

Hiroshi's jaw tightened as he absorbed the sheer scale of Rei's criminal ambitions. Weapons, cybernetics, drugs, extortion - she had her claws sunk deep into every seedy underbelly of the city.

"We also discovered intel on several high-level corporate and political insiders who were secretly working for Crimson Lotus," Himura continued grimly. "Let's just say there are going to be some major scandals breaking very soon."

Kenji let out a low whistle from where he leaned against the wall. "Akira was aiming for some serious power, wasn't she? Weapons, cyber-tech, corporate espionage - she was building an empire."

"One that's been completely dismantled," Hiroshi said with grim satisfaction. "Rei Akira's reign of terror is over, thanks to our efforts."

Himura nodded, the barest hint of a smile crossing her stern features. "You did good work out there. Though the mission's not quite finished yet..."

Rei Akira sat motionless in the stark interview room, hands cuffed to the plain metal table. Though stripped of her usual elegant attire, she retained an air of cold menace even in an orange prison jumpsuit.

On the other side of the one-way mirror, Hiroshi watched with a mixture of satisfaction and apprehension. "Are you sure having me interrogate her is a good idea, Captain? After what happened..."

Captain Himura's expression was steely. "Akira respects strength and cunning. If anyone can get through to her, it's you."

She tapped a control and her voice came through the speakers. "You have thirty minutes, Tanaka. Get whatever intel you can from her."

Taking a deep, steadying breath, Hiroshi stepped into the room and slid into the chair opposite Rei. Up close, he could make out the faint scars crisscrossing her hands and forearms - mementos of her many battles.

Rei's icy blue eyes flicked up to meet his, entirely devoid of fear or remorse. A thin, mocking smile played across her full lips.

"Well, well... if it isn't my old friend, Hiroshi Tanaka. Though I use the term 'friend' very loosely." Her cultured voice dripped with disdain.

"Let's drop the niceties, Akira," Hiroshi said flatly. "I'm only here for one reason - to extract any remaining intel about your operations before you're shipped off to a deep, dark hole."

Rei gave a small shrug, seemingly unconcerned about her fate. "By all means, ask your questions. Though I doubt my honest little Tanaka could handle the answers."

Sliding a file across the table, Hiroshi flipped it open to reveal crime scene photos - the grisly aftermath of a Crimson Lotus gun shipment gone wrong. Broken bodies tangled in crimson sprawls.

"This was your handiwork in Miyagima District. An entire neighborhood caught in the crossfire when your goons got sloppy."

The ghastly photos didn't even make Rei flinch. "Collateral damage," she replied coolly. "It's the price of doing business in my world."

Disgust twisted Hiroshi's features. How could she be so callous about the lives she destroyed? "Those were innocent civilians - kids, families. All butchered because of your greed."

One slim shoulder rolled in an idle shrug. "I won't apologize for pursuing power by any means necessary. The world bows to those with strength, while the weak are swept aside and forgotten."

"Is that what you tell yourself to justify the atrocities?" Hiroshi demanded, struggling to keep his anger in check. "Because from where I'm sitting, you're just a sadistic criminal lashing out at anything you can't control."

Her nostrils flared slightly at the jab, but Rei's tone remained coolly dismissive. "Call me what you want, but don't delude yourself into thinking you're any different. We both know you've had to bloody your own hands more times than you can count."

Unbidden, memories of all the violence and moral compromises he'd made over his career surfaced in Hiroshi's mind. The faces of those he'd killed, beaten, betrayed - all in the name of duty.

Clenching his fists tightly, he shoved those thoughts aside. "That's where you're wrong, Akira. I fight to protect the innocent, while you slaughter them without a second thought."

Rei simply smiled that thin, infuriating smile. "Keep telling yourself that, Tanaka. We're not so different as you'd like to believe..."

Hours later, Hiroshi emerged from the interrogation room feeling emotionally drained yet somehow utterly failed to crack Rei's icy veneer. Kenji was waiting anxiously in the hall.

"Well? Did our lovely yakuza princess finally sing for you?" his friend asked hopefully.

Hiroshi shook his head, rubbing tired eyes. "Not a damn thing. She's going to let every last scrap of intel about Crimson Lotus' operations die with her."

Letting out an exasperated sigh, Kenji ran a hand through his wild hair. "Guess we shouldn't be surprised. Stubborn to the very end, that one."

"More than stubborn," Hiroshi said darkly. "Completely

without empathy or remorse. It's like she sees the whole world as just...pieces to manipulate."

Kenji must have sensed his friend's troubled thoughts. "Hey, don't beat yourself up, man. We took down Akira's entire criminal empire - that's a huge win."

"I know, but..." Hiroshi trailed off, struggling to put his unease into words. "When I looked into her eyes, I saw something cold and calculating behind them. Like she was always multiple moves ahead, just biding her time."

He clenched his fists tightly. "Akira may be locked up, but I can't shake the feeling this isn't over. That she has one last play to make."

Clapping Hiroshi on the shoulder, Kenji tried for a reassuring smile. "Then we'll just have to be ready for whatever twisted game she has planned. The Crimson Lotus's roots may run deep, but we've already severed most of them."

A voice crackled over the corridor's speakers. "Tanaka, report to Processing. Akira's being prepped for transfer to maximum security."

With a nod to Kenji, Hiroshi headed for the detention block. He had to see this through to the end, had to watch as Rei Akira was put on that armored transport under the tightest lockdown.

Only then could he truly start to let his guard down.

The reinforced steel door slid open with a clang. Rei stood in the center of the stark chamber, wrists and ankles shackled. Two stone-faced guards flanked her, gripping sleek rifles.

Despite her restraints and downtrodden state, she looked utterly unbroken. In fact, a slight smile seemed to tug at the corners of her full red lips as Hiroshi entered.

"Well, if it isn't my favorite...what did you call me? 'Sadistic criminal?'" Her mocking tone rang out as the door ground shut behind him. "Come to bid me a dramatic farewell?"

Hiroshi steeled himself against the taunting lilt of her voice. "This is just the start of your sentence, Akira. You're going away for a very long time."

"We'll see about that," she replied coolly. "Things have a habit of unfolding in rather...unexpected ways. Even for the mighty Hiroshi Tanaka."

Before he could respond, the radio on one guard's shoulder crackled with static. "Incoming emergency traffic - shots fired in the east corridor! All units, get hot and—"

The transmission dissolved into screams and wild gunfire. Rei's eyes flashed with something predatory.

In one blindingly swift motion, she lashed out with her cuffed hands, catching the first guard across the throat. As he choked and staggered back, she twisted with leonine grace, whipping the chains towards the other guard.

The steel links cracked against the side of his head with brutal force. He dropped like a puppet with severed strings.

Hiroshi went for his sidearm, but Rei was already pressing her attack. She slammed her shoulder into his sternum, driving him back against the wall. Her bound hands locked around his wrist in an iron grip.

"Did you really think it would be that easy?" she hissed, her face just inches from his. Wild alarms began blaring through the corridor. "That your third-rate police force could hold me?"

With a savage wrench, she twisted Hiroshi's arm up in a brutal joint lock. White-hot agony lanced up from his shoulder as he felt it start to dislocate.

Gritting his teeth, he tried to break the hold, but she only wrenched harder. He could smell her intoxicating ruby red perfume, see the flecks of gold in her cold blue eyes.

"You're as tenacious as a virus, Akira," Hiroshi growled through the pain. "But this is your last gasp. There's no way out for you now."

Rei actually laughed at that, low and mocking. "You give me far too little credit, Tanaka. This was all accounted for...every possibility, every contingency."

Her mouth was a breath away from his ear, making the fine hairs on his neck prickle. "The Crimson Lotus's roots burrow far deeper than you could ever fathom."

Then she was shoving him away with disdainful force. Hiroshi slammed back against the wall, sucking in ragged breaths as his dislocated arm hung limply at his side.

More gunfire erupted from outside, rapidly getting closer. Rei simply stood there, looking almost serene despite the chaos and her restraints.

The door burst open in a shower of sparks. A hulking figure filled the smoke-wreathed opening, automatic rifle leveled...

The armored figure advanced through the haze of smoke, assault rifle sweeping the room. Hiroshi tensed, clutching his useless arm as more of Rei's militants poured in behind their leader.

"Well, well..." Rei purred, seemingly unperturbed by the arrival of her reinforcements. "I was wondering when you'd make your appearance, Itsuko."

Captain Himura stepped into the harsh glare of the emergency lighting, eyes blazing behind her riot mask. "This is your final mistake, Akira. Surrender immediately or we will open fire!"

The woman simply laughed, a low, mocking sound. "You're outmatched at every turn. Can't you see that?" With a subtle hand gesture, her gunmen instantly covered Hiroshi in a lattice of laser sights.

"Let him go," Himura snarled, shouldering her rifle. "Your fight is with me now."

Shaking her head in feigned disappointment, Rei tsked softly. "Always playing the stubborn hero to the last. That blind arrogance is why you and your pathetic police force could never defeat me."

With each passing second, more of the woman's forces arrived – sleek gunmen in cutting-edge cyber-armor, hulking shock troopers cradling heavy weapons. They fanned out with chilling precision, securing every possible exit and entrance.

It was then that Hiroshi saw the slight variation in Rei's movements, the way she favored her right side in those few fleeting moments. Studying her carefully, he realized she was subtly tapping out coded instructions on her thigh in binary morse.

His eyes widened in sudden realization. "Himura, she's not just stalling – she's summoning reinforcements! More troops, weapons, an extraction team! We're being boxed in from multiple angles!"

The captain's scowling features went taut with grim understanding. Shouting terse orders, she and her squads rapidly redeployed in layered cross-fire positions, snapping up portable barricades.

Bullets began pinging off the makeshift fortifications as the first wave of Rei's forces attacked. Himura's tactical visor flickered with frantic diagnostics as she consulted her team's limited stocks of ammo and ordnance.

"Tanaka, get to cover and sit tight!" she barked over the rising crescendo of gunfire. "My teams are issuing a general alert to all TKPD units. We'll buy you as much time as we can!"

But even as she spoke, the ominous thud of heavy artillery fire erupted outside. The entire cell block shook from the thunderous impacts raining down from above.

"Time's up, Captain," Rei declared with absolute confidence. "Did you really think I wouldn't plan for every contingency? That I'd make your mistake of underestimating my reach?"

Himura's jaw tightened, but Hiroshi could see the reluctant acceptance in her eyes. They were surrounded and cut off from any chance of backup or support.

As if on cue, a series of contained detonations ripped through the outer facility. The hellish barrage intensified, merciless and unrelenting. Rei's commando elites finally smashed through the last of Himura's defenses in a storm of high-caliber fire.

Dropping a thick smoke canister, Rei turned in one sinuous motion and slipped from her restraints with disturbing ease. In the churning gray haze, she moved with predatory grace toward Hiroshi's battered form.

"How...?" he rasped, scarcely able to believe what he was seeing unfold. "This whole time, you were controlling the board behind the scenes."

"Of course," she replied, that same superior smile curving her full lips. "The winds of chaos can be a powerful ally to those with the will to seize them."

Crouching beside him, Rei leaned in uncomfortably close. Hiroshi could make out every fleck of gold in her cold blue eyes, smell the metallic tang of spent ordnance mingling with her ruby perfume.

"Don't worry, we'll have our reckoning soon enough." Her whisper was almost gentle as she traced the fresh scar along his cheek with one fingertip. "I still have such...grand plans for you, my friend."

Then she straightened fluidly and rejoined her lieutenant, who was waiting with a gleaming cybernetic case. Rei removed a high-tech metal vial from the case and unstoppable it.

Bright emerald bio-illuminants swirled within the vial in viscous eddies, casting an otherworldly pulsating glow across Rei's striking features. She tilted her head back, exposing the smooth line of her slender throat as she upended the searing chemical cocktail with one practiced motion.

Streams of vivid green bioluminescence flooded into her body through specialised sub-dermal ports. Her eyes shone with raw power, lips parted in what seemed like ecstasy as the alien energies surged through her.

"What...what are you doing?" Hiroshi demanded, watching in horrified fascination.

Rei didn't answer at first. She simply allowed the ethereal transformation to complete its course as arcane cyber-circuits writhed into pulsing life across her pale flesh.

When she finally spoke, her voice resonated with a profound, glacial menace that made Hiroshi's blood freeze in his veins.

"Transcending," she intoned. "Becoming something... more."

Then an explosion tore through the room, shattering reinforced bulkheads and raining down shrapnel. Hiroshi shielded his face as the shockwave sent debris skating across the floor in a lethal hail.

When the smoke finally cleared, Rei and her entire force were gone. Vanished without a trace, leaving only Himura's battered squad blinking in stunned confusion.

Kenji came scrambling through the shattered doorway, eyes wide at the sheer scale of devastation. "Hiroshi! You're still alive!" Spotting his friend's wounds, he hurried over and helped brace the dislocated arm. "What the hell happened here?"

Grimacing through the pain, Hiroshi could only stare at the gaping breach torn through the facility's outer walls. "She escaped," he rasped in a hollow tone. "Akira's gone...and she's more dangerous than ever before."

As medics swarmed in to help treat the wounded, Kenji shot his friend a deeply troubled look. For once, the brilliant hacker seemed utterly at a loss.

"How?" he asked simply. "How did she orchestrate all of this from inside a hardened cell? It's like...like she's always multiple moves ahead of us all."

Hiroshi didn't have any answers. All he could do was look out over the smoldering ruins of the once-formidable detention block, and feel a terrible sense of looming dread.

The real fight against Rei Akira and her Crimson Lotus was only just beginning...

Hours later, Hiroshi sat in grim silence while Captain Himura detailed the full extent of the damage from Rei Akira's brazen escape. Kenji leaned against the wall nearby, arms folded tightly as he absorbed every chilling detail.

"Our outermost defensive perimeter was breached by a concentrated artillery barrage and multiple simultaneous insider attacks," Himura stated in a toneless voice. "The detention block was hardened against any conceivable assault, but Akira's forces implemented newly-acquired military-grade ordnance and cyber-warfare tactics."

She shook her head slowly, an uncharacteristic weariness seeping into her usual rigid professionalism. "By the time my teams rallied and regained control of the facility, Akira and her main strike force had already withdrawn through the egress points they'd created."

Pulling up a series of diagrams, the captain traced the staggeringly complex movements of the attack with a laser pointer. "We're still analyzing the data, but it appears her operation incorporated hijacked TKPD subnet security overrides, high-frequency ECM jamming, and next-gen viral subversion of our combat systems."

Hiroshi's jaw clenched tightly as the web of flawless coordination and meticulous planning emerged. Every component of Rei's assault had been designed to strip away each of their defensive advantages piece by piece, clearing her path with surgical precision.

"She played us completely," Kenji said in a low, disbelieving tone. "Akira made our top-rated security look like a joke without even breaking a sweat."

"Indeed," Himura replied grimly. "And the most disturbing fact is that her forces disappeared from our sensors less than eight minutes after initiating their assault." Her mouth formed a tight line behind the screen. "Whoever was orchestrating this operation has access to elite cyber-soldiers and bleeding-edge technologies that shouldn't even exist."

Dragging a tired hand down his face, Hiroshi tried to make sense of the tangle of facts and suspicions whirling through his mind. "Those compounds she injected herself with during the escape... What the hell were they?"

Himura's jaw tightened fractionally. "An extremely virulent and unstable cybernetic mutogen - something our lab techs are still struggling to identify. Early analyses suggest it granted Akira unprecedented bio-systems interfacing alongside massively augmented physiological potential."

Her lips compressed into a flat line. "Simply put, she's

operating on an entirely different level now. A true cyber-evolution, if you will."

"Like some kinda...hyper-augmented meta-human?" Kenji shook his head in a mixture of awe and dread. "Where does she get her hands on this kinda tech? It's light-years beyond anything I've ever seen!"

"That," Himura stated with grim finality, "is what we have to find out before Akira can make her next move. Because one thing is certain - this was merely a opening salvo in her grander offensive."

A weighty silence fell over the room as the three allies considered the terrifying implications. Just when they thought they'd finally excised the threat of the Crimson Lotus, the serpent had molted into something infinitely more formidable.

Finally, Kenji broke the stillness with a resigned sigh. "Well, I guess we know what our next move has to be." His mouth formed a wan smile as he glanced between his friends. "Unless you two are ready to quit while we're behind?"

Despite the bone-deep fatigue and lingering aches from his injuries, Hiroshi felt a familiar determination harden within him. No matter what terrible new incarnation she took, Rei Akira's reign of terror over Tokyo would end - one way or another.

"Not a chance," he stated firmly, meeting Kenji's gaze with an emphatic nod. "We've got a city to save...and a viper to put down for good this time."

Captain Himura allowed herself a fleeting ghost of a smile at their resilience. "Then let's get started, gentlemen. We've got a long road ahead of us."

As they began compiling all available intel and resources, Hiroshi couldn't help but feel a nagging sense of dark portent.

He kept seeing those haunting glimpses from their final clash replaying in his mind's eye:

Rei's face contorted in what seemed like agonized ecstasy as exotic cybernetic energies flooded her body. The profound, inhuman menace saturating her voice as she declared her "transcendence."

And those final, chilling words spoken amidst the destruction - a promise laden with vicious, unspoken threats.

"We'll have our reckoning soon enough…"

As night fell over the battered city, Hiroshi gazed out over Tokyo's vast neon sprawl and felt an ominous chill. Though they'd struck a major blow against Rei Akira's criminal empire, he couldn't shake the certainty that this supreme battle was only just beginning.

The Crimson Lotus's roots had only been pruned for now. Soon, that malignant force would blossom anew with a virulent hunger for domination over Tokyo's streets.

When it did, Hiroshi vowed he would be ready to sear those twisted blossoms from the earth. No matter how powerful and self-evolved Akira became, he would put an end to her madness once and for all.

The weeks passed with frantic preparation as Hiroshi, Kenji, and their allies scoured every lead and informant for any shred of intel on Rei Akira's whereabouts. The cyber-queen had gone completely off the grid, disappearing into the shadows like a mirage.

But they all knew it was only a matter of time before she resurfaced with new machinations to seize control of Tokyo's underworld. Steadily, the TKPD's cyber-crime units intercepted disturbing signs of her lingering influence.

Newly-virulent strains of digital warfare plagued the city's networks, crippling vital infrastructure and sowing chaos. Splinter factions of cyber-mercenaries and shadow corporations pledged allegiance to Akira's vision, uniting under her glowing crimson insignia. Untraceable arms shipments of bleeding-edge cyber-ordnance flowed onto the streets.

It was as if the Crimson Lotus was germinating again from deep underground, slowly spreading its crimson offshoots into every dark corner of the city. Only this time, its growth had mutated into something far more malignant and difficult to eradicate.

Eventually, a forensic cyberpath from the TKPD managed to partially decode fragments of one of Akira's lingering subversion viruses. What little data they could reconstruct revealed multiple nested sequences of cyber-alchemical code – arcane commands inputting complex routines, recursively rewriting themselves with each iteration.

Kenji spent days analyzing the code through every lens of cyber-science, his perpetual frown deepening with each incomprehensible layer he unraveled.

"Whatever mastery of esoteric cyber-physics Akira has evolved, it's far beyond my abilities to decode fully," he admitted, rubbing exhausted eyes. "It's like...she's achieved a sort of technological enlightenment. Transcended the boundaries of normal digital architecture and operating logic."

Hiroshi slammed his fist on the table, making the computer displays shudder. "So we're back to square one? No leads, no way to anticipate her next strike?"

"Not quite," Kenji replied, worrying his lower lip pensively. "From what I can decipher, these code-sequences seem to be constructing a massive, multi-nodal framework of some kind -

almost like an archetypal set of digital roots, or a cyber-conduit system."

He sat back, staring at the indecipherable alien ciphers crawling across his screen. "Whatever Rei's planning, it's going to be huge. A widespread digital ecosystem, forming piece-by-piece under our very noses."

Himura's jaw tightened grimly. "Then our top priority must be severing those roots before Akira's new paradigm can fully take hold over the city." She glanced at Hiroshi, her obsidian eyes smoldering with fierce resolve. "By any means necessary."

The hunt intensified like never before. Every available operative and asset was leveraged in a desperate gambit to pinpoint the source of Akira's subterranean cyber-machinations. But always, the cunning viper remained one step ahead - an inscrutable digital specter leaving only phantoms of code and whispers of her return.

Just when Hiroshi thought they were running out of leads entirely, a chance encounter at a shadowy underworld TP-Spa provided their first solid clue in weeks. A hacker known only as Kitsune accessed the Spa's forbidden datastream - a cyber-realm where the city's elite information brokers trafficked secrets and illicit services.

The digital avatar they encountered was stunning - a crimson-tressed, curvaceous figure robed in cybernetic silks and diaphanous biosynthetic auras. When she finally acknowledged Kitsune's intrusion into her cloistered realm, her mocking laughter echoed across realms of virtuality.

"Well, well...if it isn't the vaunted TKPD's adorable little code-monkeys come sniffing in the shadows." Her mocking tones were unmistakable, the voice of their old nemesis dripping with derisive amusement. "Tell me, are you enjoying the little puzzle-box I've constructed for your amusement?"

Before Kitsune could react, the avatar shifted and contorted in reverse mimicry - features rippling and coalescing into a nightmarish cross-hybridization of Rei Akira and something profoundly...other. Something no longer remotely human, yet still retaining her core essence.

Towering over them, the abominate metamorphosis opened its multitudinous, unblinking eyes and gazed down at them with cold, cosmic appraisal. When it spoke, its resonance made the entire datastream convulse and splinter.

"You only delay the inevitable fruition of my grand design. Soon, all your paltry human conceits of order and governance shall be subsumed by my virulent expansions..."

And that was when the unthinkable override command pulsed out like a shockwave - instantly annihilating Kitsune's avatar from within while inflicting cascades of cyber-trauma on the operator's biological matrix.

Hissing through ruined vocoders, the eldritch monstrosity that had been Rei Akira let loose one final warning before departing in a cyclone of fractal dissolution:

"Brace yourselves, insects...for the Age of Crimson Rapture is nigh!"

Hiroshi awoke from virtual stasis shaking and drenched in sweat, the harrowing subliminal images of Akira's transcendent evolution burning in his mind. Kenji crouched beside him, face pale and stricken. Behind them, medics tended to the ghastly trauma Kitsune had suffered.

As the hacker's rasping, distorted howls echoed through the staging room, Hiroshi understood that whatever unspeakable new kingdom Rei sought to birth upon the world, its gestation could no longer be prevented.

With dawning horror, he realized their window to excise the Crimson Lotus had closed. Now, all they could do was prepare for the alien seed's imminent spawning - and devise a way to survive the nightmarish paradigm about to be unleashed upon their reality.

The Age of Crimson Rapture was coming...and if they didn't evolve to face it, all of Tokyo would be its first blossoms to be reaped.